Shafted

or

The Toastrack Enigma

Shafted, or The Toastrack Enigma

An Edgar Rowdey Cape Cod Mystery

CJ Verburg

Contents

*Cover design by Barbara Oplinger
(https://boplinger.com)
The typeface is Gorey.
The framed drawing is by Meyer
from an untraceable engraving
of Metacom, or Metacomet,
the 17-century Wampanoag sachem
who was given the English name
of Philip (later called King Philip).*

Many Thanks to Everyone Who Helped

starting with Edward Gorey and Jack Braginton-Smith,
my original and much-missed co-conspirators on the
Edgar Rowdey Cape Cod mysteries,
with special thanks to Edward for "The Toastrack Enigma"

➤

My deepest gratitude to Carol Wynne, Ramona Peters,
Paula Peters, Courtney Powell, David Pocknett, Curtis Frye,
and the other Mashpee Wampanoag Tribe members who
generously supplied information, insight, and advice.
If I've misconstrued anything, I apologize.

➤

Thanks also to Rick Jones and Gregory Hischak at
the Edward Gorey House,
my Mechanics' Institute writers group comrades
Patricia Dusenbury, Eileen Hirst, Mike Norris,
Kathleen Poole, and Michael Ryder,
the Mashpee Wampanoag Indian Museum, Mashpee
Wampanoag Police Department, Mashpee Public Library,
and Falmouth Public Library,
Peter Vanderwaart, Bonnie Verburg, Brenda Reinertson,
Margo Pisacano, Mary Nelson,
Yolanda Fletcher, and Mary Zeile Dill,
and the organizers, speakers, and sponsors of
Bridgewater State University's
Here It Began: 2020 Hindsight or Foresight
Indigenous History Conference.

The
Toastrack Enigma
D. Andrew Gore

Chapter 1: The Morning After

"Come on, man." Mudge jabbed his thumb at the men's room. "You made the mess, you clean it up."

Tony Harrington blinked at him blearily from behind the cash register. His feet were wrapped tight around the rungs of his stool, as if it were a rodeo horse that might try to buck him off.

How old was this pest? Young enough to be his son. Too young to boss him around in his own dad's restaurant.

Old enough to drink? Stupid question. The kid's pulling in a paycheck. He's an Indian. This is Cape Cod. Of course he drinks.

So why can't he recognize a killer hangover?

Tony blinked again. *Go away, pest!* His eyes were having trouble focusing on Mudge's lean brown arms and white apron moving back and forth in front of him. He felt seasick, the pounding pain in his head churning up his stomach.

A window of horror opened in Tony's mind. He slammed it shut.

You're fine. No worries. You're fine. No worries.

"No worries," he muttered. "'S my place."

That came out wrong. But Tony couldn't explain that if he tried to re-cross the twenty feet from here to the men's room, he'd fall over and crack his head, or heave his guts on the floor, or both.

A voice like a gunshot pierced his skull. "The hell it is. Last time I checked, sign out front said Leo's Back End. Your name Leo?"

Dinah, the cook. Tony didn't twist around toward the kitchen. Even when he hadn't recently polished off a fifth of 30-year-old Scotch, Dinah Rowan was an unsettling sight. Rolls of chin like a stack of inner tubes. Arms the size of a beef haunch. Beady little eyes peering out from her pink pillow of a face.

Shut up, fatso!

"You do look kinda like a Back End. Here. Drink this." A ceramic mug landed on the counter with an ear-jarring clunk. "Then go clean up after yourself. Just 'cause you're the boss's son don't mean you can get away with murder."

Tony jerked convulsively. He covered by reaching for the mug. Make her think it's the prospect of facing his dad that shook him.

So smug, these small-town hash-slingers. So sure they knew why screw-up Tony drank himself under the rug last night, ha ha! Dinah left before yesterday's meltdown, but Leo —who lived upstairs—would've heard all about it from Mudge and that punk chick Lydia.

So, yeah. When Leo came down in two hours, he'd be unbearable.

Only for once in his life Tony didn't care. Leo was a tiny drop in the shit-bucket of trouble he was already in.

If I could've just left well enough alone. Stuck with the plan. Oh, God in heaven, if I could just please God turn back the goddamn clock.

He chugged Dinah's concoction. It tasted like stewed rubber boots. If (as he expected) he lost his cookies again, he'd blame her. But after a few minutes his nausea ebbed. At the first break between customers, Tony staggered back to the men's room.

No worries. You're fine. No worries. You're fine.
Yeah, right.

>→

Lydia Vivaldi fingered the second stud in her right earlobe. No surprise Tony spent last night getting shit-faced. The question was, how? Celebrating a deal with his new business partners, or drowning his sorrows alone?

She hoped the luncheon he'd hosted here yesterday had paid off. If GreenHome LLC hired Harrington Associates, that would be a coup the whole Back End could celebrate. Tony could quit griping to anyone who'd listen about wasting his talents in a greasy spoon at the back end of nowhere. Leo could quit griping at Tony about ingratitude. Dinah could quit yelling at both of them to shut up. Lydia wouldn't have to dodge Tony's playful hands when she passed the register. And Mudge could take back his favorite job of ringing up customers, honking the horn when someone dropped change in the tip pot and clanging the bell for folding green.

Not to mention, if Harrington Associates landed a paying client, Tony couldn't weasel out of paying the balance he owed Lydia and Mudge's catering start-up, the Flying Wedge.

They'd given him a gourmet feast on a fast-food budget: the chowder thick with clams, the salads crisp and fresh, all three kinds of sandwiches devoured down to the crumbs. Mudge's warm-from-the-oven Rowdeyberry Tarte melted ice cream without burning anyone's mouth. Rosalie Gerber—daughter of GreenHome CEO Brad Gerber—actually grabbed Mudge's arm to thank him for his brilliant cranberry-corn muffins.

Tony hadn't thanked anybody for anything. His party had started dispersing before Lydia realized they were through with their coffee. She didn't expect Tony to hang around and give her and Mudge a full report, but how about some appreciation? He didn't even thank his dad, Dinah said, although this was the first time in history Leo ever let anybody use his restaurant for a private party.

She'd wondered about that just now, riding her bike down the long driveway from Main Street and across the Back End parking lot. Did Tony hold a grudge because customers kept asking how much longer he'd be sitting in for Mudge as Leo's cashier? He always laughed it off—*summer rush can't last forever!* Still, Lydia could see it galled him. Tony was an attractive, personable guy—curly dark hair, blue eyes, tanned and toned from daily runs on the shoreline path, always joking with the kids and old ladies—but Mudge was half his age and twice as hot.

That didn't stop Tony from flirting with every woman who walked through the door. Lydia braced herself as she took her apron off its hook. If he'd pulled off his deal yesterday, he'd hustle over and bear-pounce: wrap her in a hug, smother her with promises of more gigs for the Flying Wedge. If he hadn't, he would badger-pounce: *Why was Harriet Benbow looking for you in the kitchen? Did Mudge hear anything from the Wampa-noags? What did Rosalie Gerber want besides muffins?*

Lydia had resolved not to open any of those cans of worms. Now she wouldn't have to. Tony was in no shape to pounce on anybody.

"Hey." Mudge rounded the corner with a tray on his shoulder. "The Flying Wedge rules!"

"Hey." Lydia pumped a fist and nodded at the men's room. "Did you get that from the horse's mouth? Along with a fat roll of cash, by any chance?"

"No roll of cash. I got that from my cousins. Mr. T's doing the other end of the horse."

"He swore yesterday, full payment before the bank closes at

noon. He better not even think about stiffing us."

"No worries." Mudge flashed his trademark grin. "We've got the whole Mashpee Wampanoag tribe on our side."

They delivered breakfasts to tables and headed back to the kitchen. *I am so lucky to know you, Kevin Mudjekeewis Miles,* Lydia thought, *before the outside world discovers you and you leave this place in the dust.*

"So what did your cousins say?" she asked him.

"I didn't see Carl. Red Otter said we're genius. He wants me to open a restaurant in Mashpee. I said, Sure. We'll call it No Reservations."

Lydia chuckled. Good they could still joke about the federal government's vacillations over the Wampanoags' legal status. That had started long before she arrived in Quansett —400 years ago, in fact, when the Pilgrims landed on Cape Cod. Carl must be the smooth but edgy one of yesterday's pair, the tribal executive. She couldn't remember his title or last name. His silent partner she remembered vividly. Chief Red Otter's silver-streaked black hair hung in a braid down his back from a spray of eagle feathers. His burly chest had been bare except for a fringed buckskin vest and a shell-and-bead necklace. When he and Carl stopped by the kitchen to greet Mudge, Lydia had noticed a tomahawk hanging from his belt.

Trust Harriet Benbow to seat herself next to the Indian chief.

No. You are not thinking about Harriet Benbow.

Because Harriet didn't belong in the picturesque village of Quansett. She was an alien invader from a planet Lydia Vivaldi had left behind almost four months ago, when she crossed the Sagamore Bridge and became a soup-chef and all-purpose staffer at Leo's Back End.

It wasn't until Harriet started talking yesterday that Lydia had recognized her. The lady with round sunglasses, masses of dark curls, and a flowered Lilly Pulitzer sundress who'd breezed through the door with Tony didn't ring any bells. But that voice! All the way from the back room it jolted her: a confident yet intimate mezzo soprano hinting that she was the one person in the world you could trust to share your secrets.

Tony had kicked off his business luncheon with an unexpectedly charming speech about choosing a homey setting instead of some trendy but sterile spot that clashed with the spirit of their collaboration. What collaboration? Something about real estate. For the first few minutes Lydia had tried to eavesdrop *(what the hell is she doing here?)*, but that ended when lunch got under way.

She'd stayed out of sight as best she could. It didn't work. When Mudge went around the table filling coffee cups, she heard Harriet's voice in the kitchen doorway: "Liz Valentine, isn't it?"

She looked up. Giant poppies and white teeth blocked the only exit.

"Nope. Sorry."

"From Cambridge. One of my groups. I'm quicker with faces than names, I'm afraid."

"Lydia Vivaldi. I live here in Quansett."

Harriet's smile didn't falter. "Well, it's good to see you, Lydia. You look wonderful. And your cooking, oh my God! Congratulations."

"Thanks."

That was that. Lydia's hands hadn't stopped shaking for several minutes, but it didn't matter, with everything pretty much done except clean-up.

Leo had popped his head in after Tony and his guests departed. Lydia told him Mudge needed to leave for his other job, but she could wait around for Tony. Leo said no need, clapped them both on the back, said he'd see them tomorrow, and handed them each a twenty-dollar bill.

Lydia was so exhausted by the time she climbed into her loft bed that she slept for ten hours.

Judging from his bloodshot eyes and zombie grimace, Tony didn't.

>→

"Hey, Kev," said Mudge, stacking plates on the counter.

"Hey, Kev," said Officer Kevin Kelly. He deposited his stocky self on a formica-and-chrome stool and his hat on another.

A day when Officer Kelly didn't get his coffee break until 11:25 was a day to hope you had no outstanding traffic violations. His scowl sent Lydia retreating to the soup tureens.

Dinah claimed it was Mudge's fault that Quansett's local cop hung out at Leo's. Though the two Kevins had known each other in high school, they ran with different crowds. No one guessed back then that Kevin Kelly would go into law enforcement. And until Kevin Miles started using his middle name and working at the Back End, no one guessed that (a) he had a gift for pastry, or (b) his apple-ginger coffeecake would hook Kevin Kelly.

Dinah slid over a mug of coffee. She'd seen that scowl.

Mudge set down a spicy golden-brown cube topped with streusel. "'Sup, Kev?"

"Suspicious death." Kevin Kelly chomped off a chunk.

The kitchen went still. After five seconds Leo sidled out from the grill, gaunt and white-haired in his splotched white apron. He asked "What happened?" just as Dinah asked, "Anybody we know?"

Kevin Kelly mumbled: "Under investigation."

One of the other coffee-drinkers at the counter spoke up. "That don't sound good."

Another regular asked, "Where's this at?"

"SailPort Landing."

Glances rippled around the room. SailPort Landing was the new condo development going up on Fishhook Point. By next summer it was meant to be a gated waterfront community, but right now it consisted of three model townhouses overlooking a salt marsh. The only move-ins had been a truckload of saplings, each with an ID tag stating its intended location and affirming it was personally selected by the project's landscape architect.

"Who's dead?" Leo asked.

"Can't tell you."

"Who found the body?" asked Dinah.

"Realtor." Kevin Kelly chewed and slurped. "Goes in to show the place, trips over the victim."

Questions were coming from all directions now. Victim: did that mean this was a murder? When did it happen? Was it in one of the townhouses? Where was the body now? Who was handling the investigation?

Lydia, watching him gobble his coffeecake, asked, "What did you see?"

"Blood." Officer Kelly grimaced. "A lot of blood."

Chapter 2: Trouble

Four miles away, Louise French stood at the kitchen sink in a model townhome at SailPort Landing scrubbing her shoes.

Didn't some character do this in a play? *Out out damn spot.* Or, no. That was hands. Louise's hands were next in line for a stiff antibacterial scrub. Soon as she got the damn blood off her Manolo Blahniks.

The agents' tour was down the toilet, obviously. Her assistant had given everyone a quick look at the other two units, but how much could she accomplish with Emergency Rescue due any minute?

Thank God these were her colleagues and not clients.

Showing to prospective buyers, Louise preferred to wait in her car. Walk them up to the front door and stand back so they could enter first. *It's their dream home you want them stepping into, not yours,* she'd explained to the officer who answered her call. He didn't get it—didn't listen, really. What does a twenty-something beat cop know or care about real estate? The tactics, the shoes, the Mercedes convertible. In her job, first impressions were make-or-break. In his job, she supposed they were usually a smokescreen.

Trouble. That's what had hit Louise like a sledgehammer at Two Harbor Lane. Not *bloody dead person on floor.* By the time her brain caught up with her reflexes, she'd been inches from stepping on the deceased.

Behind her, through the open front door, she could see

the first arrivals parking their cars, walking toward the slate-paved path. Quick, call 9-1-1. State her name, the address. Then hurry down the driveway with a smile and a wave: *Welcome to SailPort Landing! Sorry, last-minute glitch, can't get into the Ketch right now, but you'll love the Yawl and the Sloop.*

Her assistant had taken over as tour guide. Louise retreated inside, locked the door, sent an urgent text, and prayed (successfully) that everybody would leave before sirens came roaring through the gate.

Thank God the media hadn't followed them. Yet.

She'd glanced only one more time at the nightmare in the hall. As soon as the last car drove away, she hurried across the lawn to the Yawl, on tiptoes so her heels wouldn't sink into the sod. She had to get out of here. Erase the image in her head. Catch her breath before the police arrived full of questions.

What she should do was call Brad Gerber.

And her office. Louise French was legendary for turning lemons into lemonade, but there were rules about disclosure, not to mention a hyperactive local grapevine, and no way was she going to list a home where someone had just met a violent death.

"Just" and "violent" being the problem. In a village as old as Quansett, ghosts came with the territory. Louise had once sold a sagging sea captain's mansion for 20K over asking to a pair of historians eager to share it with the widow who walked under the full moon.

But Two Harbor Lane was no antique. It was a brand-new townhome with stainless steel appliances, granite countertops, and an eco-friendly bamboo floor which almost certainly would have to be replaced.

"Louise."

Walking toward her was Exmouth Police Detective Pete

Altman.

"Pete. Thanks for coming over." This might be OK. Louise had sold Pete and Jenna Altman their house as newlyweds. Now it was worth three times what they'd paid for it.

"Thank you for the heads-up. How you doing?"

"I'm OK." Louise smiled up at him, small but brave in her stocking feet, wiping a spike heel with a dishtowel. "Not sure about these."

"I'm so sorry. CIO's still in there," Pete tilted his shaggy salt-and-pepper head toward the Ketch, "photographing and so forth. I'm afraid it'll be off limits for a while yet. You found her, is that right?"

She nodded. "Is she . . .?"

"Yeah. Beyond help. Nothing you could have done."

"How did it happen?"

"That I can't tell you. The medical examiner's on his way."

Louise put on her shoes. Pete steered her through a sliding glass door onto the deck.

"You knew her, did you? The deceased?"

Louise's insides froze up. She nodded, but she couldn't speak.

Pete went back inside for a glass of water. They rested their elbows on the wooden railing, side by side, looking out past the narrow fringe of woods to the salt marsh below which linked the SailPort Landing site with Fishhook Cove and Cape Cod Bay. Louise kept her eyes off the deck next door, draped in yellow crime-scene tape.

"Pete, do you think— Who could have done that? I know, you can't tell me. But . . ." She shuddered. "Like an animal attack."

"Try and put it out of your mind, OK? Help me with the facts. Was this lady a friend of yours?"

After a sip of water Louise answered, "She was a business

acquaintance. Harriet Benbow. She—oh dear. She worked for GreenHome LLC. I really should call Brad Gerber."

"And she was on the property to do what?" Pete gazed down at the marsh, green and gold and russet in the September sun.

"I don't know. I suppose . . . This is a difficult weekend for them. Brad and Rosalie. His daughter. They're hosting a memorial service tomorrow for his late wife, Lanie, Rosalie's mom. I suppose Harriet probably came by to check on the townhomes."

"She didn't live here?"

"No. Nobody lives here. These are three model condos they offer to prospective SailPort Landing buyers. We're in the Yawl. That one is the Ketch, and the smaller one next door is the Sloop."

"Who is Brad Gerber?"

"The CEO of GreenHome. The project developer? You'd recognize him—big blond guy. Golfs every Thursday at the Yacht Club. Harriet was his business manager. She started out as Lanie's assistant when her cancer came back. So sad! I've known them forever. Lanie and Brad and little Rosalie. Not so little anymore. Anyhow. After Lanie passed, Brad told me GreenHome might rethink SailPort Landing. In fact it was Harriet Benbow who said Brad wanted to explore the option of selling off the three model townhomes."

"So you came over to show them to a buyer?"

"Oh, no. This was an agents' preview. I offered to bring in some of the top producers from our sister offices, get their reaction." At Pete's inquiring look, Louise explained: "SailPort Landing was planned as twenty-eight units: nine groups of three, like this one, and a clubhouse. GreenHome's had the land for ages. But when values shot up, so did wetlands restrictions. Lanie was sure once they got these first three units through, the rest would follow. Brad wasn't convinced. I think he hung on through all the legal wrangling mostly for her sake. Now she's gone . . ."

"Can't beat the location." Pete shaded his eyes to peer through the glass door. "Alarm system?"

"Oh yes. Automatic lighting, and CCTV, and you saw the gate out front."

"So nobody should have been in there." He faced her. "What about this unit here and the other one?"

"Also empty. With the open house, naturally we checked them all top to bottom."

"You call this empty?" He waved a hand. "Electricity, water—?"

"You can't show a home without lights, Pete. Or running water. Believe me."

"But, furniture? Pictures on the wall? Towels in the bathroom? Pots and pans on the stove?"

"Staging. Buyers respond best if it looks cozy but classy. You know? Walk right into your perfect new life."

"Sounds like Goldilocks."

That brought back Louise's smile. "If Goldilocks read *House and Garden*."

"Any idea how Harriet Benbow got in?"

"There's a key in the lock-box on each front door. She'd just punch in the passcode."

"Do you have the passcode?"

"Sure." Louise repeated what she'd told the officer who was first on the scene. "What I do is, I always ring the bell first, even if I know it's empty. Open the lock-box, take out the key, unlock the door. 'Hello?' It was dark inside after the bright sun, so I didn't see— I could only see there was a shape on the floor. Until . . ."

She stopped. Pete Altman waited.

"You think your eyes are playing tricks. I didn't scream or anything. I thought, Omigod, there's people right behind me. So I called 9-1-1, and my assistant: *Get over here quick!* I was pretty sure, you know, what you said. She was beyond help. I didn't try— I went back out, locked the door, and sent everybody to see the other two units." She looked up at Pete. "I need to call Brad Gerber."

"Leave that to me." He patted her shoulder. "You done good, Louise."

"They always say, don't touch anything." She gave her head a vigorous toss as if to shake out the memory.

"That's right," said Pete. "One last question. You've been in that townhouse before? When was the last time you went upstairs?"

"Oh, gosh. We finished the staging around ten days ago, and then the cleaners . . . Earlier this week. Wednesday? Tuesday? I like to check personally before anyone else sees it. Upstairs, downstairs— It's a funny thing. Women always want to start with the bedrooms, and men want to start with the basement. Why do you ask?"

Pete Altman's phone pinged. "Excuse me." He looked at the screen; pressed a key. "The medical examiner's here." He ushered her back inside, through the open living area and out the front door. "Thanks, Louise. You take care now."

She waved goodbye from her car. Altman walked across the freshly sodded lawn to meet the van and see if the Criminal Identification Officers could answer his next question: *Who's been sleeping in Papa Bear's bed?*

Chapter 3: Treasure

The sight of Officer Kevin Kelly having coffee at the counter jolted Tony out of his stupor. Lydia seized her chance to liberate the Flying Wedge's balance due. She ran up Main Street, cash in hand, just before the Congregational Church's bells struck twelve: closing time for the bank, starting time for the Back End's noon rush. Almost time for her favorite customer to arrive.

Off Cape, Edgar Rowdey was renowned as the probably British, probably dead, definitely weird author of creepy little black-and-white storybooks. To Quansett he was a kind-hearted old eccentric. Lydia lived in his guest cottage, and she could testify that while Edgar's heart was kind, and his thin frame and white beard bore a slight resemblance to George Bernard Shaw's, he was neither British nor dead. His chief weirdnesses, as she saw it, were: A, he was a bona fide genius; B, yet he'd quit Manhattan for this sleepy seaside village; and C, he ate nearly all his breakfasts and lunches at Leo's Back End.

Usually Edgar Rowdey greeted whoever was up front, moseyed over to check the Speshuls taped to the wall, wrote his order on a slip, and then meandered off to his table in the back room with a paperback book. Today he halted at the register.

"I've been yard-saling!" he caroled.

Tony winced.

Edgar placed a small shopping bag fussily on the counter. Leo glowered at him from the kitchen. "What the fork is that?"

He'd just lectured his staff about language: Tony at the register, Dinah at the grill, Lydia and Mudge delivering orders, and Bruno, who didn't speak English, loading the dishwasher. *No more gol-darn cussing! This is a family restaurant, dang it!*

Dinah, the chief offender, snorted and went on flipping burgers. As the Back End's cook, she was irreplaceable. They all were, really, given Leo's pay scale. The true purpose of these rants was to entertain the customers. *You don't come here for the food,* Lydia had been told on her first visit. Four months later, she'd grown to enjoy the snarky banter that drew in enough tourists as well as locals to keep this place afloat.

Leo edged out past Officer Kelly, who'd ordered a sandwich to go when he realized he might not get another break anytime soon. Edgar made a show of hunching over his shopping bag, as if to defend it from attack.

"You gonna pull out a rabbit out of there?" Leo challenged. "You see the sign up front? No animals in a food-service facility!"

"It's a service rabbit," someone quipped.

A fist thumped the counter. "Show me the bunny!"

Edgar reached into the bag. Lydia held her breath. *Oh God please not a kitten!* Everyone in Quansett knew that Edgar Rowdey never turned away a homeless cat. Last time she'd checked, the feline count in his rambling old house was five.

"Today's Speshul, fricaseed hare!" someone called.

Out of a crumpled-newspaper nest came an object the size of a football. No mewing; no struggle. *Thank you God!* He peeled back the comics section and held up his prize.

"I repeat," said Leo. "What the fork is that?"

Edgar lifted a disdainful eyebrow. "Isn't it obvious?"

Dinah made a sound between a grunt and a chuckle.

"Oh, sure. An Early American Obvious. I'll tell you something, old coot. You been watching too much Antiques Road Show."

Lydia sidled in closer. Edgar's new treasure was round on top and flat on the bottom, maybe six inches long and five inches tall. Five parallel silver hoops arched like barrel staves over a rectangular base. Topping the middle hoop was a two-inch handle shaped like the outline of a spade in a deck of cards.

"It's a rack for file folders, right?" said Officer Kelly. "Goes on your desk."

"If you're thinking I'd put order slips in there, think again," Leo said. "They'd fall right out."

Edgar Rowdey heaved a martyr's sigh.

"That pointy loop on top looks like a bottle-opener," Mudge offered.

Another sigh from Edgar.

"Oh, for fork's sake," said Lydia. "It's a toastrack! What the fudge kind of a breakfast joint is this? It's gorgeous, Edgar. Art Deco, right? Did you seriously find that at a yard sale?"

He beamed at her.

"A toast rack?" Dinah didn't believe it.

"They're big in England," said Lydia. "Your toast goes in the slots, and they carry it to your table by the pointy handle. To make sure your toast will be stone cold when you butter it."

"That's why they invented English muffins?" Mudge turned over the toastrack curiously.

"Now, of course you're all wondering—"

Edgar halted in mid-sentence. Lydia felt the whole front room stiffen, as if a skunk had wandered into a family picnic.

Officer Kevin Kelly spoke. "Sir. I'm just getting a sandwich."

On this hot Saturday afternoon, Exmouth Police Detective Pete Altman looked more like a golfer than a cop: plaid short-sleeve shirt, khaki pants, beat-up running shoes. He wasn't even wearing his usual jacket and concealed shoulder holster.

"Good afternoon, detective." Leo wiped a hand on his apron to shake. "What can we do for you?"

"Leo. How's it going?"

Edgar carried his toastrack to the fireplace and cleared a space for it among the knicknacks on the mantelpiece. With a nod to Altman, he withdrew to the order-slips podium.

"Mind if I ask you and your staff a few questions?"

"What for?" Leo shot back. "Somebody dead?"

"About a private party you had in here yesterday."

Lydia glanced at the cash register. Tony was gone.

"In case you didn't notice, my staff is busy serving our distinguished clientele."

"Well, here's the thing. This is meant to be my afternoon off, and I promised my grandkids I'd take 'em to the Ospreys game."

Leo's mouth twisted. "We offer a discount to members of local law enforcement, if you're hungry."

Pete Altman took the stool at the counter beside Officer Kelly, who whisked away his hat just in time.

Mudge caught Lydia's eye. She tilted her head at the register and raised an eyebrow. Mudge nodded, set down his tray, and sauntered toward the men's room.

Dinah ambled over from the grill. "Hey, Pete. What'll it be?"

"How about a piece of your best pie?"

"You're in luck. I got one slice left of Rowdeyberry Tarte."

She brought it topped with whipped cream and accompanied by a mug of coffee. There was a suspenseful silence while Detective Altman ate. Then he continued to Dinah: "This private lunch yesterday. Did you cook for that?"

"No sirree. My afternoon off? You won't catch me hanging around here."

"So who fed them? Leo?"

"Ask Leo."

Lydia handed Officer Kelly a brown bag. "Mudge and I did," she told the detective. "We want to start a catering service."

They'd agreed that until they got around to the paperwork—licenses, insurance, regulations—the Flying Wedge would operate on a need-to-know basis.

"Aha. And where is Mudge?"

He emerged from the men's room, smiling and wary. A flick of an eyebrow told Lydia he hadn't found Tony.

"Hey, detective."

Although the desserts he created for the Back End were buffing up his reputation, Mudge's colorful youth had included several clashes with the police. He was still—as Leo's youngest and darkest employee—a cop magnet.

Pete Altman pointed his fork at the soft peaks of cream melting into purple berries and crumbling chunks of crust. "This is— Amazing. You made this?"

"Yeah." Mudge visibly relaxed.

"So," Leo cut in, "who's dead?"

Their stalemate might have lasted several minutes—*I'll ask the questions, I asked you first, I'm a police officer, You're in my restaurant*—if not for the empty stool at the cash register. Somebody had to ring up customers. When Leo stepped in, the Back End regulars wanted to know what happened to Tony. Was he the reason why there were two cops in here? Perp or victim? Or had he succumbed to food poisoning or some disease they should be informed about?

"What, you lost too many brain cells to recognize a hangover?" Leo retorted.

"Find Tony Harrington," Detective Altman told Officer Kelly. "Leo, what's he driving?"

Kevin Kelly radioed in an alert for a late-model red Mustang and took off in his cruiser. Pete Altman dropped a folded bill in the tip bucket and told Leo not to let any of the staff leave until he came back.

Lydia was stirring the soups in the back room when Edgar Rowdey called: "Yoo-hoo! Waitress!"

He'd finished his Chix Pot Pi. However, the Back End didn't have waitresses. If a customer wanted his table cleared, his coffee refilled, or a clean dessert fork, he could do it himself.

Edgar laid down the book he'd been reading. "I take it our detective friend has gone off?" As if Altman were a spoiled pint of cream.

"For now." Lydia read the book cover upside down: *SIMENON Un crime en Hollande.* "Leo won't let him grill us during business hours."

"Did he reveal what this is in aid of?"

"He asked about Tony's luncheon yesterday. And now Tony's disappeared. Altman sent Kevin Kelly after him. He wants to come back and question us over staff lunch."

"Mm." Edgar frowned.

"What are you thinking?"

"Oh, the worst, as always. Would you care to dine tonight? I hear that new seafood place at Barnstable Harbor is quite zippy. Early Bird Specials and all." He picked up his book. "If you're free."

"Like, not in jail?"

Too late: Edgar had returned to French and the Netherlands.

"A bientot," said Lydia.

Chapter 4: Questions

Pete Altman returned to the Back End at 2:20. With the last leftovers stowed and customers gone, he asked Leo, Dinah, Lydia, Mudge, and Bruno to bring their lunches to the big round table in the back room, the scene of yesterday's party.

No, Tony hadn't turned up yet. Yes, Detective Altman could now confirm that a fatality had occurred. He regretted to inform them that Harriet Benbow, a Cambridge resident employed by GreenHome LLC of Sandwich, had been found dead at SailPort Landing here in Quansett.

Uneasy glances darted around the table. The whole point of a waterfront luxury development was to offer pleasure and sanctuary to those who could pay for it. Even the *No Trespassing* signs posted on SailPort Landing's chain-link fence promised to keep out trouble. Shouldn't that include fatalities?

Lydia avoided Mudge's eyes. "What happened?" she asked.

"It's got nothing to do with Tony," Leo stated.

"Don't go blaming the food," said Dinah.

"I'm not blaming anybody," said Pete Altman. "We don't know what happened. That's all I'm trying to do, is find out. First step, trace Ms. Benbow's movements. You all remember seeing her here yesterday?

They did—Dinah and Bruno just for a few minutes, Leo for close to half an hour, Lydia and Mudge for the hour-plus of Tony's luncheon.

"How did she seem? Enjoying herself? Any complaints? Disagreements?"

"She had a wonderful time," Leo declared. "Same as all our guests at the Back End. Whatever happened later, it didn't start here."

"OK, then. Let's look at the timeline—"

"Hold it, detective. How did this lady die? Somebody whacked her? Is that what you're saying?"

"No, Leo. I'm not saying anything. It's way too early. We don't like to speculate ahead of the evidence, and I hope you won't, either. Obviously, since I'm here talking to you, we're looking into it as a suspicious death. That doesn't mean we suspect anybody of anything. It means we don't know."

"Who found her?"

"Let me repeat, this is a police inquiry. I'm here to get answers from you, not the other way round."

Leo snorted.

"Having said that, Ms. Benbow's body was discovered this morning in an empty townhouse, one of the model condos at SailPort Landing. I'm telling you because you'll hear soon enough, it was Louise French who found her."

Dinah grimaced at Leo. Louise French's real-estate office was up on Main Street, across the parking lot from the Back End.

"She's pretty shaken up. You won't want to make it worse by pestering her."

"I never pestered anybody in my life," said Leo virtuously.

"OK then." Detective Altman took out a pocket notebook and a pencil. "Two PM yesterday. Tony's party was here, at this table?"

"Right," said Mudge.

"You don't need Bruno for this," Leo said.

"Fair enough."

Leo made shooing motions at Bruno, who grabbed his plate and scrambled off. Altman was drawing a circle, marking where everyone had sat: Tony at twelve o'clock, with his back to the windows, facing toward the kitchen. Brad Gerber on his left, Harriet Benbow on his right. Rosalie Gerber had sat between her father and Carl Hammond. Then came Red Otter, next to Harriet Benbow.

The detective placed a recording device in the middle of the table. "Orders from the top," he explained. He tapped his notebook: "I do better with this, myself."

Lydia saw Dinah's mouth twitch: *Yeah, sure you do.*

"Later on I'll want to talk to each of you individually, but I'm hoping we can save some time if we run through the sequence of events together."

He started with simple questions. *Who got here first?* Tony, with Harriet Benbow and Rosalie Gerber. He'd offered to pick them up early for a guided tour of historic Quansett. Brad Gerber was invited, too, but he had a golf date with some old friends who'd come down for tomorrow's scattering of his late wife's ashes at sea.

"Tomorrow, meaning today," Leo clarified. "From the family yacht."

"Not much of a yacht," Dinah said. "Forty-five-foot schooner."

"You let them go ahead with that?" Lydia asked Pete Altman.

"Sure. Why not?" He looked at her across his notebook. "No point stopping their memorial because they've lost someone else. Did anybody mention this ash-scattering yesterday?"

"Not that I heard. But I wasn't listening. I was cooking."

"Did you hear anything else that they talked about?"

Before Lydia could answer, Mudge stepped in. "Real

estate."

"What in particular?"

"Donno." He shrugged. "Like she said, we were too busy to listen."

Leo said, "Harriet Benbow thanked Tony when they all sat down for taking their minds off a sad occasion. And then Tony gave a toast. To Lanie Gerber."

"What exactly did he say?"

The sounds of doors closing and footsteps approaching made everyone turn to look.

"You talking about me?" asked Tony Harrington.

➤

Tony leaned against the shelves of crockery and condiments that divided the front and back rooms. Though he was striving for his usual cocky tone, his voice sagged with a weariness that matched his strained face and his rumpled hair and clothes.

Leo rose. "Where the hell you been?"

"I needed some fresh air."

Officer Kevin Kelly leaned around him. "Detective? You want him here or down at the station?"

"Here's good. Where'd you find him?"

"Barnstable Harbor. Cleaning out his car in the parking lot. I collected the plastic bag out of the trash bin."

"Good. Did he resist?"

"No sir. But . . ." He looked around the table. "Can I speak to you a second?"

"You folks stay here, OK?" said Detective Altman, and led Officer Kelly out the front door.

Tony would have taken Bruno's empty chair, but Leo blocked him. "What the Hellman's Mayo was that about? I kick out my own paying customers at the peak of a busy Friday afternoon—"

"Hey," Dinah growled.

"—and this is the thanks I get? First you show up for work late, looking like a zombie—"

"Leo!" When Dinah rose from her seat, anyone within arm's length had to step back. "Give him a break." She turned to Tony. "You! Sit down and shut up, you hear me?"

Tony sat.

Leo stuck out his chin at her. "Now, listen here—"

"Shut up. You listen to me, you old fool. You got two cops out there looking to pin a murder on somebody."

"Pete Altman just said—"

"You want your son in the hot seat?" Dinah loomed threateningly. "'Cause that's where he is. So how's about you quit squawking and get him out?"

"OK," Detective Altman's voice came down the hall before the rest of him. "Officer Kelly's heading on back to the station. Tony, you want to go with him, or stay here and help me with my inquiries?"

"Here's good."

"OK, well then, I need you up front for a second. Why don't we take a three-minute break. I know I could use a sandwich, and I'm betting so could Tony."

Leo would have followed them into the men's room if Dinah hadn't steered him off to the kitchen. Mudge phoned the Frigate bookstore to say he might be late for his afternoon shift. Lydia carried empty plates to the dishwasher. She'd never heard the Back End so silent.

When they reconvened at the round table, Tony was wearing red canvas boating pants and Topsiders. From his grim expression, Lydia guessed he'd have traded his Mustang for a large Scotch.

"What more can I tell you?" he asked Pete Altman. "Like I told Kev—Officer Kelly—I'm totally in shock. I didn't know Harriet Benbow very well, but I liked her, and I looked forward to working with her. Her death is a terrible tragedy. A blow for me personally, and much worse for my company."

"Tell me again why you took off out of here."

Tony grimaced. "I guess I just lost it. I spent yesterday morning showing her and Rosalie Gerber around Quansett. The old town pier, the shipyard, the common, Captain's Row . . . We hit a couple yard sales, got lemonade at the apothecary's . . . And then I hosted them here for lunch, along with Brad and our two guests from the Wampanoag community."

"Did you go out for drinks with Ms. Benbow last night? Or any of these people?"

"No, I did not."

"I heard you came in to work pretty hung over."

"My own fault. I'd been under a lot of stress, and I guess I let it all out last night."

"Alone?"

"Yup. Just me and a fifth of single-malt Scotch."

"Better eat your lunch, then." Tony had only taken two bites from his Tooner Sallid Samwich. "But tell me first. This company of yours."

"Harrington Associates. We're expediters for off-Cape enterprises that want to do business here. That aren't familiar with our local process."

"Like, consultants?"

"Exactly." Tony bit into his sandwich.

Dinah said, "Wash-ashores hire them to cut through the red tape."

"More than that." He swallowed. "We help our clients with location scouting and acquisition, scheduling, permits, contractors, hiring, the whole nine yards."

"Gotcha," said Pete Altman. "And what was your project with Harriet Benbow?"

"I'm not sure I can legally tell you that."

"Well now, Tony, let me assure you that you can."

There was a pause. Tony ran a finger along his temple, under the tips of his curly dark hair, wiping away little beads of sweat.

"I hoped to collaborate with GreenHome on several projects. Starting with SailPort Landing."

Chapter 5: Inventory

There was a moment's pause. Would Dinah repeat her quip from yesterday? *If you think the high-rollers who did Duxbury Commons and Emerald City Wareham are gonna hire Tony Harrington to grease their wheels for SailPort Landing, you got your head up your orifice.*

She didn't. Dinah dodged any trap that might keep her here after closing.

"Let's run through your guest list again," Pete Altman said to Tony. "We've got you, the host, and Ms. Benbow, business manager for GreenHome LLC, and who else?"

"Brad Gerber, GreenHome's CEO, and his daughter Rosalie, VP in charge of operations. Then we had Wampanoag Tribal Council Chair Carl Hammond and Chief Red Otter."

"Huh. Is the tribe involved with SailPort Landing?"

"Not that I'm aware of. Harriet—Ms. Benbow—asked me if I'd include those two gentlemen in our luncheon, and I said sure, no problem. My understanding was, she wanted to get to know them better, for whatever reason, and I was happy to help. That's what I do."

"Thank you." Pete Altman turned. "Mudge, can you add anything about this? Dealings between the Mashpee Wampanoag tribe and GreenHome LLC, or Harriet Benbow specifically?"

"No."

"You know Mr. Hammond and Mr.—Red Otter?"

"Sure. They're my cousins."

"But you don't know what they might have been discussing?"

Mudge hesitated. Then he shook his head. "If I did, I couldn't tell you without asking them."

"Gotcha. OK, then. One more thing. Is there any particular reason why your cousins have different kinds of names?"

This time Mudge's hesitation was to figure out how to explain. "We all have different names. An Anglo name for outside stuff, like school and driver's license—we get that when we're born. Our Indian name is more about who we are, so that can change. Like, Red Otter decided to use that name when he got elected chief. Carl Hammond uses his Anglo name since he works a lot with outsiders."

"Aha. Thank you." Pete Altman made notes. "Now, back to our timetable." He flipped a page. "Tony. I understand you arrived here first yesterday, with Harriet Benbow and Rosalie Gerber. Walk me through that."

"Sure. I picked up Harriet at ten-thirty. I'd invited—"

"Wait," said Altman. "You picked her up where?"

"SailPort Landing. She was staying in one of the model condos."

"I thought nobody lived there."

"Harriet wanted to try it out. You know she lives—she lived in Cambridge, but she had this five AM memorial thing yesterday in Quansett. For Lanie Gerber, Brad's late wife."

"Mrs. Gerber died, what, six months ago?"

"That's right. Yesterday would have been her birthday. She'd requested Brad and Rosalie to sprinkle some of her ashes in the garden at sunrise. Before they scatter the rest at sea."

"This afternoon, off the family yacht." Pete Altman checked his watch. "Right about now."

A shadow of Tony's old smile appeared. "I'll take your word for it, detective."

"You weren't invited?"

"It's a small yacht."

"So you picked up Harriet Benbow at SailPort Landing. Did you spend the night there?"

"No, I did not."

"And which condo did you meet her at?"

"The Ketch. I don't know the address—the one closest to the salt marsh? Two bedrooms, wrap-around picture windows and deck, eco-friendly flooring and cabinetry. The other two are the Yawl and the Sloop."

Pete Altman made notes. "Did you go in?"

"I— Yes, I did, briefly. She couldn't find her cell phone. I helped her look for it. And of course I was curious, since I hoped to help GreenHome with the project."

"Did you notice anything unusual? Any sign of visitors? Anything out of place?"

"Nope. Neat as a pin."

Lydia shot a look at Dinah. Are you thinking what I'm thinking?

Dinah rose without signaling back. "Detective, you don't need me for this."

"Ms. Rowan." Pete Altman stood to face her. "I wouldn't have kept you if I didn't need you. Let's pause there for a second"—he turned to the others as he leaned in to stop the recorder—"and I'll be right back."

He gestured for Dinah to precede him to the kitchen.

With a quick look at Mudge, Lydia followed them. She eavesdropped from behind the wall near the cash register.

"Have you noticed anything missing?" Altman asked Dinah.

"Like what?"

"You tell me. Any kitchen tool that should be here and isn't. A knife, a meat hammer, a beater off an electric mixer?"

"No."

"Would you know? Say if someone ran off with one of your spatulas. How soon would you notice it was gone?"

"Soon as I went to reach for it and it wasn't there."

"Do you or Leo have an inventory?"

Dinah snorted. "Are you kidding me?"

"So, a customer could take a fancy to one item or another and slip it in his pocket? Walk out the door? No problem?"

"No problem until he come back and order what we use it for. 'Sorry, can't make your Egz Bennie, somebody poached the poachers.'" There was a five-second pause. "Is that it? I got other plans beside sit around here till the cows come home."

"Right," said Pete Altman. "I'm going to need that inventory from you on Monday. You have a good weekend, Dinah."

The front door slamming behind Dinah sent a gust of impatience through the back room. Lydia stood behind her chair as if she'd never left it, stretching ostentatiously. Mudge checked the time on his cell phone. Tony drummed his fingers on the table.

Leo jutted his chin at Pete Altman. "Habeas corpus."

"Meaning?"

"What've you got, detective? If you're investigating a murder, say so. If you're fishing, Tony will show you the pier."

Detective Altman turned on his recorder. "Leo, you weren't here for this lunch yesterday?"

"I don't interfere in my son's affairs."

"Is that a yes or no?"

"I stayed until things got rolling. Made sure the chefs had what they needed."

"That's Lydia and Mudge?"

"Yes," said Lydia.

Altman asked Leo, "What time did you leave?"

"Soon as my regular customers cleared out. Two-thirty?"

"That's right," said Tony.

"You're free to go, then, Leo."

Leo scowled, folded his arms, and stayed put.

"Suit yourself," said Altman. "Lydia. Mudge. You were here from when to when?"

"Seven AM straight through clean-up around four," said Lydia.

"And did you have everything you needed? Food? Equipment? Did you bring your own or use what was here?"

"Equipment, we used what's here," Lydia said. "We went food-shopping the night before. Mudge's sister picked up fresh bread and salad greens for us on her way to Four C's."

"I brought my own muffin tins and two knives," said Mudge.

"What kind of knives?"

"Victorinox. A six-inch and a three-inch. They're in my truck."

Pete Altman swiveled. "Tony. You drove here with Ms. Benbow and Ms. Gerber after taking them on a tour of local attractions, is that correct? Then Mr. Gerber arrived on his own, and Chief Red Otter and Mr. Hammond."

"Yes."

"How far apart?"

"Couple minutes. Not long."

"Did you all leave together?"

"The ladies left first," Tony said. "Then Red Otter. Brad and Carl Hammond and me stayed a little longer."

"Both ladies at the same time?"

"Rosalie I thought was going to the rest room. When she didn't come back, Harriet went after her. Red Otter just kind of drifted away—he hadn't said a word all afternoon. Brad told Carl he'd give him a call later, and we wrapped it up."

Pete wrote that down. Then he asked, "Lydia? Mudge? Is that how you remember it?"

"Yup," said Lydia.

"What time was this?

"Three-twenty?" Mudge said. "I work Friday and Saturday afternoons at the Frigate, so I was in kind of a hurry to clean up and go."

"I came by and shooed them out of here," said Leo. "Locked up, call it quarter to four."

"Did any of you see or speak with any of Tony's guests after that?"

Heads shook.

"OK. One last thing." Detective Altman's eyes went slowly around the table. "At any time before, after, or during this luncheon, did anybody get into a disagreement with Harriet Benbow, or take offense at something she said? Anything like that?"

For a moment nobody spoke.

"No," Tony said. "There were some differences of opinion, but that was the point. To bring together a range of views on a range of issues."

"Issues, like what?"

"Property development. Land use. One way or another, that's what it all boiled down to."

"OK," Altman nodded. "I'll need more details, but we don't have to keep these other folks hanging around. Leo, Mudge, Lydia, thanks for your cooperation."

Mudge stood up. "We can go?"

"Yes. For now. Don't leave town without telling me first. And if you can help us keep a lid on the grapevine, I'd appreciate it."

"Ha! Fat chance," said Leo.

Chapter 6: Ashes

Rich women are too damn touchy, thought Ricky Hanlon. Anybody aboard the schooner Calliope might have asked Rosalie Gerber the same question: *Why'd you bring a toy boat on a memorial cruise?* Just making conversation, since they'd be stuck out here together for the next couple hours. But she'd snapped at him: *This is the urn.* And stalked off clutching it to her bosom: a scalloped white paper sail on a chopstick mast, jutting from the balsa-wood hull that held her mother's ashes.

Aside from that bosom, Rosalie didn't look a bit like the portrait of Lanie Gerber propped on an easel below decks. Take away her fluttering black dress and Brad's Exmouth Yacht Club blazer and Rosalie was the spitting image of her dad.

Officer Hanlon stood where he could watch the mourners without being watched, behind the semicircle they formed around the Gerbers on Calliope's stern. His cover thinned when the ceremony started and people removed their hats. Out of respect or to keep them from blowing overboard? The breeze had freshened, turning their mellow afternoon brisk. Ricky Hanlon braced himself against the cabin, one hand gripping its wooden edge and the other clutching his hat, which regulations did not allow him to remove.

He'd hoped to pick up some gossip, maybe even clues, about yesterday's suspicious death. Hah! Brad Gerber had sandbagged that option by breaking out the booze as soon as

Calliope cast off. *A toast to Lanie, God bless her, the dearest, sweetest, kindest woman who ever lived.* His buddies raised plastic champagne flutes: *To Lanie! To her husband Brad, the love of her life, her partner in marriage and business. To their beloved daughter Rosalie. Hear hear!* As more corks popped, the tributes expanded: *To Harriet Benbow, who cared for Lanie on earth and now is with her in Heaven. To the fine work of GreenHome LLC. To Cape Cod! Hey, and how 'bout those Red Sox?* Most of the guests were three sheets to the wind when they reached the ash-scattering site.

Ricky Hanlon was thankful to learn that "scatter" didn't mean scatter. Brad spoke a few halting words. Rosalie read a poem she'd written, drowned out by the wind. Then she placed the little urn-boat on an oar which her dad lowered off the stern, and stood with her hands folded as it bobbed, drifted away, and disappeared.

Another round of champagne. By now whitecaps were tossing sea-spray onto the deck. With Calliope bouncing across the water like a snowboarder on a bumpy ski slope, the mourners retreated below for the voyage home.

Officer Hanlon looked forward to joining them as soon as possible. His observation post gave him a clear view from bow to stern, but it was hella cold. And wet. And right now, both ends looked like trouble.

Only the three nondrinkers had stayed on deck. At the prow a teenage boy and girl stood in the pulpit playing Kate and Leo in *Titanic*—not easy, with the schooner heeling and the jib in their way. The girl leaned into the wind like a bowsprit, shaking her hair in exhilaration. The boy had one arm wrapped around her waist and the other around the railing.

Forty feet aft, the other girl was manning the helm. Actually she was filming her friends on her phone. She'd braced a leg against the tiller to hold the boat on course, but she hadn't even glanced at the sails. Calliope had begun to shudder. If that boom swung over—

Up from belowdecks swarmed Rosalie Gerber, hollering: *What the hell? You want to sink us?*

The girl jerked back in surprise. She dropped her phone and reached down for it.

Ricky Hanlon scrambled toward the cockpit.

The boom swung. Rosalie kneed the girl aside and grabbed the tiller. Calliope heeled, wobbled, then righted herself, like a horse stumbling and recovering.

Rosalie's multi-layered skirts billowed as if she'd arrived by parachute. She didn't look much more sober than her guests down below. However, common sense had trumped mourning: under her black dress she wore rubber-soled deck shoes.

Ricky Hanlon slid in beside her. The girl and her phone fled down the companionway ladder. Kate and Leo dodged the sails, the blonde witch, and the cop, and followed her below.

"Miss Gerber. Are you OK?"

"Rosalie," she said. "I'm fine. How are you, officer?"

"Me? Good." He adjusted his hat. No reflective surface here for a man to check if he was earning his reputation as a Matt Damon lookalike, or if tufts of clown-hair were sticking out around his ears. He sat kitty-corner to her. "Your memorial celebration going OK?"

Remembering Detective Altman's list of instructions: Address everybody by their last name unless they request otherwise. Don't call it a party or a cruise; it's a memorial event or a celebration of the deceased's life. Full uniform at all times. Lend a hand if you get the chance, but don't let them forget you're there as a police officer. You'll stand out at first but soon you'll be invisible, and who knows what you might observe?

Rosalie just shrugged.

Yeah, well, Ricky Hanlon thought, same here. In an hour and a half he hadn't observed a damn thing he hadn't seen and heard at other bereavement events. *So sorry about your loss. Much loved and much missed. Anything I can do, don't hesitate.*

Two shiny-headed men emerged from below. Cans of beer in the pockets of their Exmouth Yacht Club windbreakers clanked against the companionway ladder. They nodded to Rosalie and sat across the cockpit from Officer Hanlon, popping tops, discussing baseball.

Too big a crowd for too small a boat, was the problem. Plus you had to yell over the wind. How was a would-be detective supposed to show his initiative if he couldn't even conduct a private interview?

Rosalie Gerber wasn't helping. She still looked more like a witch than a hostess, with her hair blowing all over the place, her black dress ballooning like a Genoa jib, and not a smidge of makeup. That could be grief, though. Under those freckles she had nice smooth skin. For a woman over thirty, she kept herself in damn good shape. Another place and time, like say a bar on a slow night, he might have bought her a drink.

So, Ricky. Initiative!

"I'm sorry," he said. "About, you know. Losing your mom."

Rosalie gave a little snort like a laugh mixed with a sob. "Not your fault. You didn't lose her."

"No. I meant . . ." *Nothing. Jesus. Just making small talk, OK?*

"I know what you meant. Sorry. Am I turning into a bitch? It's been a bitch of a weekend. They must have told you. About Harriet? That's why you're here, isn't it?"

"Harriet. You mean the lady who—ah—yesterday?"

"Died." Rosalie bent her head and put her hand to her face. "She died. My best friend. My mom's best friend." A sob came through her fingers. "Who never got sick. Always took care of everybody else. How could this happen?"

The two baseball fans exchanged a look, collected their beers, nodded goodbye to Officer Hanlon, and retreated back down to the cabin.

"It's horrible. Horrible! A nightmare that just won't stop." Her head swung back up. "This is going to kill my dad."

Ricky Hanlon didn't know how to respond to that, except to look sympathetic.

"A suspicious death, your detective said. What does that mean? Suspicious how? *Sorry, confidential! But don't worry, we don't suspect you. Or maybe we do. We can't tell you till we finish our paperwork! Next week? Next month?* You. Officer Hanlon, is it? You don't know my dad. Under that strong silent front, this is tearing him to pieces. Lanie, my mom, was his heart and soul. And on top of that, losing Harriet?"

"I understand. It's a terrible tragedy—"

She cut him off. "What *happened*, for God's sake? This time yesterday I almost thought we'd pull through. The three of us. How can Harriet be *gone?* Just like that?"

Rosalie was sniffling, groping for a handkerchief. Ricky Hanlon glanced from her luffing skirt to the sails. If she lost her rag again, he calculated he could reach the tiller in three seconds.

"Hey." Low voice. Soothing. "We want to find out what happened as much as you do. If you need to talk to somebody, we have—"

"How did she die? Tell me that." Fierce eyes glared into his. "Was it a heart attack? Did she fall off the deck? Did somebody break in?"

"I can't tell you. Sorry." He gulped air and wished he had a beer. "I don't know."

"The hell you don't. You—the police—took away her body."

"Miss Gerber—"

"Rosalie. Yes or no. Was she still alive when they found her? Did an ambulance come, and paramedics, and give her CPR? Did they take her to the hospital? Go ahead, tell me. I can find out. I will find out."

"No."

"No, she was already dead?"

"Yes. I'm sorry—"

"Natural causes? Accident?"

"I don't know the cause of death."

"Was there anything . . . visible? Like, injuries? Blood? Bruises? Any clue at all to what happened?"

"Don't do this, Miss Gerber. Rosalie."

"Nothing you tell me can possibly be worse than what I imagine. I beg you, officer."

He shook his head. She thrust the tiller at him, hard. The schooner swerved and tilted. The sails flapped. Shrieks echoed up the hatch stairs. Beer cans flew across the cockpit.

Ricky Hanlon lunged for the tiller and hauled Calliope back onto an even keel. Rosalie Gerber buried her face in her black skirts and wept.

Chapter 7: Hunting

For a long, breathless moment, Detective Pete Altman thought Tony Harrington was going to slug him.

So did Tony.

Leo Harrington, who'd been averting (and sometimes breaking up) fights in the Back End for half his life, leaned in to block his son's bull-like charge across the table with his own skinny frame.

Tony didn't back down, but his fists slammed wood instead of Pete Altman's jaw. "Are you arresting me?"

The detective replied in the same matter-of-fact tone he'd used throughout this interview. "Right now I'm asking you. To make a formal statement at the station, and to give us your house keys and your permission to look around."

Leo turned his ice-blue glare on Altman. "What the hell for?"

"So I don't have to waste your time and mine getting a search warrant on a weekend."

"Look around for what?" Tony asked through clenched teeth.

"Any evidence that can help us find out what happened to Harriet Benbow. And support what you've told me so far." Pete Altman flipped pages in his notebook. "You hosted a catered lunch here from two to four PM Friday, that's yesterday, for the deceased and her employers. The idea being Green-Home would hire you as their expediter on SailPort Landing and other projects. What you all discussed at this meeting, you refuse to say."

"I told you, I can't violate our nondisclosure agreement."

"You did say, Harriet Benbow arrived on Cape from Cambridge sometime the previous evening, but you didn't see her. You were home prepping for Friday's lunch. No one can confirm that. Your first meeting with Ms. Benbow was ten-thirty AM yesterday, at a supposedly empty townhouse at SailPort Landing where she'd spent Thursday night."

"Since she had to be at the Gerbers' before dawn for the private ash-scattering. Is what she told me."

"You entered the townhouse with her briefly, to look for her cell phone. The two of you were joined by Rosalie Gerber, whose home is five minutes away, and you drove around Quansett sightseeing until one-fifty PM. You met your other luncheon guests here at two," Altman tapped the table. "The six of you spent the next hour and a half discussing business which you won't tell me about, except it's related to land use and property development. You all went on your separate ways around three-thirty. You did not see Ms. Benbow again. You drove around, bought a bottle of Scotch, and spent the evening alone drinking it and writing up your notes. Is that a fair summary?"

"Yeah. Type it up and I'll sign it. Five minutes. And I want my car back."

"You'll get your car back when the forensics team is done with it. And you'll get a statement to sign when I've heard what you folks talked about at this lunch. I understand you see that information as confidential, proprietary, what have you; but it's not privileged with respect to a criminal case."

"Like I said, detective. Show me the relevance and I'll consult with my clients. My business is built on discretion. Violate a nondisclosure agreement without cause and I'd be signing my professional death warrant."

The lift of Tony's chin and the rigidity of his jaw made Detective Altman wonder if he was rehearsing for a press conference.

"Well, since you mention warrants, here's the other thing. Nobody can confirm your whereabouts from four-fifteen PM yesterday, when you left the package store, until you arrived here at seven this morning with a bad hangover. That's the same period when the crimes took place that I'm investigating. As of now, I've got possible robbery, breaking and entering, fleeing the scene, interfering with a police investigation, assault with a deadly weapon, all connected with a suspicious death which may be a homicide."

"I did not fucking kill Harriet Benbow!"

"Language!" muttered Leo.

"I didn't rob her, I didn't assault her, I didn't break and enter, and I didn't flee the scene. This is ridiculous!"

"You fled this scene." Altman sat back in his chair. "You led the police on a wild goose chase an hour ago to avoid questioning." He folded his arms. "You're a flight risk, Tony. Face it. I'd be derelict in my duty if I didn't take you in."

"I want a lawyer."

Leo stood. "I'm calling Fred Jones."

"Sure. Let me add, this is also for your own protection. Somebody committed a string of serious crimes in Quansett last night. Maybe armed, definitely dangerous. If that wasn't you, you don't want to be the next target."

Fathers of daughters, in Ricky Hanlon's experience, were a fiercely protective species. Though he didn't dare leave Calliope's helm, he kept his distance from the hysterical female beside him.

Brad Gerber's blond head and white polo-shirted shoulders erupted from the cabin like a polar bear lunging toward a seal. "What happened?" he barked.

A question Officer Hanlon was tired of hearing. He replied with a forced smile: "It's OK, sir. No worries. Sorry to disturb you."

Gerber was already half-kneeling on the cockpit cushion, wrapping his arm around his daughter. He shook her shoulders as if waking her gently from a nightmare. He murmured into her sun-bleached, wind-tousled hair.

Rosalie grew calmer. Straightened up. Mopped her eyes with the handkerchief Ricky Hanlon had traded her for Calliope's tiller.

"It's my fault," she sniffed. "I can just hear Harriet: *Rosalie, you are not coping effectively.*"

"Harriet, dammit." He sighed. "Of all the times . . . Officer Hanlon," he swiveled. "What progress have your people made?"

"Mr. Gerber, we only got this a couple hours ago. We don't have much yet."

"He won't even tell me how she died." Rosalie's voice quavered.

"Until the autopsy's done, it'd be guesswork," Ricky Hanlon said.

"That's not strictly true," said Brad Gerber. "Priorities, wouldn't you say?"

"Theirs against ours," Rosalie muttered into his shoulder.

"You're out to find the facts, and at the same time, build a case that'll stand up in court. Dot your I's and cross your T's. Yes?"

"Yes, sir, exactly," said Ricky Hanlon. "Don't jump the gun, is what they tell us, or the case goes down the tube."

"In sailing it's Loose lips sink ships. Like, for example, say

I knew what happened to Harriet. You, the police, would want me to keep that under my hat until you get your autopsy results."

"For sure." Officer Hanlon gulped.

Rosalie sat up to face her father. "Do you mean that? You know how Harriet died?"

"Later." He rubbed her arm. "This afternoon is for your mother."

He was frowning, but not at her. He squinted past the cockpit at the sea and the distant shore ahead. "Where are we? Where's what's-his-name? Winslow?"

"Seasick," said Rosalie. "His kids took over—"

"We're way the hell off course." He took the tiller from Ricky Hanlon. "You sail? Good. Go uncleat the jib. Rosalie, get the main sheet."

Another blonde head popped up from the cabin: not windblown but smoothly pulled back in a chignon. "There you are! Rosalie, dear, I've looked everywhere. And isn't that Ricky Hanlon? Officer Hanlon, I should say."

"Hey, Mrs. French." His parents still claimed they owed Louise French their retirement condo. Seeing her familiar friendly face was such a relief that when his hat tried again to blow away, Officer Hanlon tossed it into the cockpit.

Clambering forward, he couldn't hear their voices. Damn! Did Brad Gerber mean that? How could he know what happened to Harriet Benbow? He must have talked to Mrs. French, who'd found the body. Had she described what she saw? That wasn't the same, though, as Rosalie's question: How did Harriet Benbow die? Not even the police knew that.

It looked from here like they'd changed the subject. To what? Weird how much you could and couldn't tell, watching people talk without sound. He saw Rosalie make an emphatic point which Brad disagreed with. He saw Brad present a counter-argument which Rosalie rejected. He saw Louise French hear them both out in attentive silence. When she finally spoke, she smiled at each of them, touching an arm or a shoulder as if asking for advice. Ricky Hanlon knew from here it was Louise's proposal they adopted.

Made you think twice about trusting witness statements.

Rosalie bunched up her skirts and descended the companionway ladder. Her father—reasserting himself as Calliope's skipper—beckoned Ricky Hanlon back to the cockpit. Instead of fighting this wind, he explained, they would run with it: Sail toward Hyannis, into the lee of Great Island, and then back home along the shore. Give Lanie's loved ones—especially the out-of-towners—not just a farewell cruise, but a tour of the Cape landscapes she'd loved.

Their daughter had gone below to round up the guests. Officer Hanlon needed to understand what a rough day this was for her. Rosalie was one hell of a brave gal, a sportswoman through and through. Even as a kid she'd play injured rather than complain. But inside? Losing her mom and now her best friend was killing her.

"With your help, she'll pull through." Louise French patted his arm. "You're so right, Brad. She's all you on the outside and all Lanie underneath. A stoic with a soft heart. It won't be quick and it won't be easy, but Rosalie's a trooper. She'll come out on top. You both will."

"Once this is over," Brad nodded. "Once we get back on course."

"SailPort Landing," said Louise. "She'll be glad to see Lanie's legacy carried out at last."

"Harriet's legacy, too, now." Brad Gerber leaned over. "Officer, you need some help there?"

Ricky Hanlon had stooped to retrieve his hat. Not wanting to interrupt them, he'd stayed on the cockpit floor. But invisibility wasn't an option when you were crawling between two pairs of legs.

"Sir, no thanks. Just looking for a stud off my hat. I think it fell through the cracks."

"Don't rush it," Louise told Brad. "Take all the time you need."

"It's more a question of, should we hold back on account of all this, or is now the time to move forward?"

"You don't have to decide that today."

"You're on board with the idea, though?"

"I think— I don't want to bias you. But, yes. This could be the answer you've been looking for. Two birds with one stone."

"Lanie's universal solvent." He let out a shuddering sigh. "If only . . . "

"The timing," Louise agreed. "Tragic. Heartbreaking."

Ricky Hanlon brushed imaginary dirt off his hat. Voices floating up the companionway ladder meant Rosalie must have corralled her guests.

"Maybe this is exactly the day to make a decision," Brad said.

"Your call," said Louise. "We'll talk later. Here come your friends."

Damn! Ricky Hanlon thought as he straightened up. And also: *Finally!* His knees were killing him.

Chapter 8: Mashpee

Back in the long-ago days before last Spring, before Lydia Vivaldi fled the ruins of her life in Cambridge to find a new one on Cape Cod, she'd scorned naps. Sleeping in broad daylight was for the weak: drunkards, babies, cats, old people.

Working at the Back End had turned her into a nap junkie.

Some afternoons she'd hop on her bike after closing and ride straight to a beach where she could spread out her towel and crash. So much of the Cape was shoreline that the hardest part was choosing: Ocean or lake? Wooded, rock-strewn, or sandy?

On this hot Saturday Lydia defied a direct police order by pedaling across the town line. After two super-intense work days, she craved privacy. With Labor Day past, even Mayflower —the most popular beach on Cape Cod Bay—wouldn't be blanketed with tourists. Where better to decompress before her dinner date with Edgar Rowdey?

Only her brain wouldn't shut off.

Somebody's killed Harriet Benbow. They must have. Or why enough blood to shock Officer Kelly? Why all the questions from Detective Altman?

She jogged along the water's edge, in and out of the shallows. *Why did I refuse to talk to her yesterday? Why didn't I just ask her what she was doing in Quansett?* Easy: *Because I wanted her to not be here.*

Presto! Gone.

Lydia splashed out to waist-high water and swam. *Anyway, I knew what she was doing here.* How had Tony phrased it? *Land use and property development.* Evidently while Liz Valentine of Cambridge was morphing into Lydia Vivaldi of Quansett, Harriet Benbow had morphed from a professional counselor into GreenHome LLC's business manager.

So? She was crap as a therapist.

Stop, Lydia! Let it go. You barely knew her. This is not your fault.

It's my problem, though, she answered herself. *What if Harriet told Tony that his dad's soup-chef came to her for help back when Liz Valentine was a woman on the verge of a nervous breakdown?*

Would Tony have told Leo?

Would either of them tell Detective Altman?

What was *she* going to tell Detective Altman? He'd be back at Leo's on Monday, and this time he wouldn't be pitching softballs.

How much should she open up about any of this? Not just Harriet Benbow, but the roller-coaster discussion at Tony's lunch? She and Mudge had stretched the truth when they said they were too busy to listen. Did they owe it to Detective Altman to report what they'd heard? And seen?

Step One: emergency conference with Mudge.

Step Two: dinner with Quansett's resident genius, Edgar Rowdey.

Twenty-five miles away, the man whose order Lydia was flouting pulled his cruiser into a parking space. This asphalt lot was almost as long as Mayflower Beach and as new as the Mashpee Wampanoag Tribe Community and Government

Center it fronted. A small cluster of cars huddled around each freshly planted tree, as if hoping it would grow fast enough to offer some shade.

Under normal circumstances, Detective Pete Altman would have invited Carl Hammond and Red Otter to the Exmouth Police Station. These weren't normal circumstances.

He'd asked Hammond on the phone if he could drop by with a few questions regarding a suspicious death. They both knew this wouldn't become an official murder investigation until he got the autopsy report. But Pete Altman didn't need a medical examiner to tell him Harriet Benbow could not possibly have bashed herself from collarbone to scalp, knocked herself out, bled all over the floor, and disposed of her weapon before expiring.

There was a strong chance her killer hadn't left Cape Cod. How much of a threat did that pose to others? Hard to say. In Altman's experience, anyone who has taken a life is a dangerous person. Whether Ms. Benbow had disturbed an intruder, clashed with an ex-client, or pissed off somebody at Tony Harrington's lunch, her death had been brutal. Best to err on the side of caution.

That went for every part of this case. One thing you had to give Tony: his guest list (the base for Altman's Persons of Interest list) reeked of clout. The two surviving partners in GreenHome LLC? The two top leaders of the Mashpee Wampanoag tribe?

Brad and Rosalie Gerber, thankfully, were too busy with their ash-scattering ceremony and houseful of guests to require his attention until Monday. His team had sealed the SailPort Landing condo and gotten Brad's OK on security. Ricky Hanlon would keep an eye on Calliope.

That left Carl Hammond and Red Otter.

He assumed they were the tribe's top leaders. A Native

American tribe was a sovereign nation, legally speaking. Did that make the chief and the head of the tribal council heads of state? Pete Altman was familiar (too familiar, in his view) with the complications of dealing with corporate bigwigs. He had no idea what kind of structure Red Otter and Carl Hammond fit into, much less what their job descriptions were. How did that impact the case? He wasn't sure, exactly. As far as he could ascertain, nobody was sure, exactly.

Standard procedure on Cape Cod was quirky anyhow. Each town had its own variations, which its police force tended to regard as the one and only proper way of operating. In Altman's Town of Exmouth, if a corpse turned up in Quansett or another of the town's four villages, it would be investigated by one of Exmouth's police detectives in partnership with one of the state's. Not on Wampanoag territory. The Commonwealth of Massachusetts had no jurisdiction here. That being the case, winning federal recognition meant the tribe had to hire its own police force. *A small one,* said Altman's buddy in Mashpee. *They expect to coordinate with us and other towns.* How small? One and a half men: Chief Rodney Cargill and his cousin Roger, who split his time with the Town of Mashpee force. But then the Wampanoags' reservation in Mashpee was small: about 150 acres when you added all the parcels together. Less than a quarter of a square mile.

Pete Altman's drive here from Exmouth had taken him through long stretches of the same Cape Cod scrub that surrounded this building: stubby wind-stunted pine trees choked with brush. An arched arcade laid a stripe of shade from the parking lot to the front doors. He followed it into a round glass-walled lobby that could have housed a large carousel.

Stepping inside the Community and Government Center, he became invisible. That was an odd sensation when he was on duty, even in plain clothes. Altman was far enough from his home turf that he didn't expect to be recognized, but he'd braced for some reaction—alarm? deference? hostility? These people barely glanced at him. Women and men, children and teens, middle-agers and seniors—everyone seemed to be heading somewhere, although not in a hurry. Faces lit up as they greeted each other: *Hey, cousin! How's your sister's baby doing? Have you seen granddad this week? Did auntie get over that flu?*

A cheerful brown teenager with purple hair escorted him down a hall and up some stairs to Carl Hammond's office. The chairs were so new they smelled like a furniture showroom. Pete Altman couldn't see what kind of desk Hammond had, buried under stacks of paper and miscellaneous objects— rocks, chunks of antler or petrified wood.

The Tribal Council Chairman rose. His grip was strong, his manner friendly but reserved. Pete Altman took in his powder-blue cotton shirt and pressed jeans and guessed: forty-plus, business degree, works out. His black hair was combed straight back and held in place with some shiny substance that made Altman curious to touch it.

Interviewing was a lot like fishing, in Pete Altman's experience. Start in the right place, prepare your approach carefully, and proceed with patience and cunning. Carl Hammond reminded him of the wily old trout who lurks in a deep pool, sometimes sighted but never caught.

"Are we waiting for Chief Red Otter?"

"The chief can't join us today."

"I'm sorry to hear that. Thanks for seeing me on the weekend." Altman sat. His chair gave a small sigh and sank an inch under his weight. "Nice place you got here."

"Our roof is shaped like a turtle shell. The terrazzo floor downstairs? Wampum. Seven hundred pounds of quahog shells, broken up by our people." Carl Hammond leaned back, lacing his fingers behind his head. His hair didn't move. "Ten, twelve, fourteen thousand years we lived here. Four hundred years we struggled not to lose our homeland. Then, magic! Somebody signs a document and we officially exist. Suddenly we need infrastructure. Offices. Meeting rooms. A gym. A cafeteria. Laws. Protocols. Phone numbers. Email addresses. All this?" He waved his arm around the room. "Went up in six months."

"You serve meals here?"

"Oh yah. We look after our people. The folks who got rich developing our land? Wasn't us."

"You're changing that now."

"As best we can. Healthy food for the elders and kids. Affordable housing."

"Thanks to the casino deal?"

"Not yet. Soon. Maybe. The casino deal made us a more attractive investment. More grants and loans, less smoke and mirrors."

"How does GreenHome LLC fit into that picture?"

Carl Hammond considered for a moment. "I wouldn't say that they do. For the tribe, I would say GreenHome fits into a different picture. Also clouded by the I.R.A., but not so much."

"The I.R.A." It rang a faint bell. "Remind me . . .?"

"The Indian Reorganization Act of 1934. Congress's attempt to say once and for all who is legally a tribe. It stated that members must have been under federal jurisdiction at some previous time—that is, living on a reservation. The Mashpee Wampanoags were never completely removed from our land."

"So no reservation."

"No. Our sovereignty here has been recognized since the first Europeans arrived." Hammond spoke matter-of-factly.

"Many experts spent many years debating whether that counted as tribal status. In 2007 the United States government accepted that it did. Only their I.R.A. required us to create a reservation. Taking that unusual step opened new legal questions."

A big fat can of worms, as Altman recalled. "Gotcha," he said.

"Now resolved, we hope. We always hope."

"That's been a sticking point for your casino, right?"

"Among other things."

"And GreenHome?"

"Stepped back." A thin smile. "Not to cloud the picture."

"Did you talk about that at Tony Harrington's lunch?"

"No."

"How about afterwards? I understand you and Chief Red Otter left soon after Rosalie Gerber and Harriet Benbow. Is that correct?"

"Ah. Your suspicious death. Yes, that is correct, and no, the chief and I did not have any discussion with those two ladies."

"Did you come straight back here?"

"Detective Altman. Is this now a homicide investigation?"

"No, Mr. Hammond. Not at this point. I'm trying to trace Ms. Benbow's movements after your lunch together in Quansett. Where she went, who she had contact with, what was on her mind."

"I'm afraid I can't help you."

Altman opened his notebook. "I'm sorry about your loss. Seeing as you had business with Harriet Benbow, and you'd just shared a meal with her . . ."

"Thank you. Coming so soon after Lanie Gerber's passing, yes. It's a shock."

"Can I ask how you heard about it?"

A faint smile. "Smoke signals?" He held up a cell phone.

The detective shot a bright smile back at him. "Mr. Hammond, you're a busy man and so am I. Let's see how quick I can run through my questions and get out of your way."

Was it Mudge Miles who'd passed along the news of Harriet Benbow's death? Yes, Hammond confirmed. Mudge had phoned Red Otter, who relayed the message but didn't care to talk about it.

We'll see about that, thought Pete Altman.

How well had Chief Red Otter and Mr. Hammond known Ms. Benbow before yesterday's lunch? That was a leading question, and Hammond ducked it: They both were honored by Mr. Harrington's invitation. They were pleased he chose a caterer from their tribe. They welcomed a chance to renew their ties with GreenHome. They were encouraged by Ms. Benbow's commitment to their late friend Lanie Gerber's priorities and projects.

"What exactly was GreenHome working on with the Mashpee Wampanoags?"

Hammond didn't respond immediately. "I like to think that we helped GreenHome to find its identity. Our paths crossed more than once over the years. Spending time on Cape Cod, the Gerbers saw how lightly our people lived here. They saw how well the land thrives when it is shared in harmony by all the beings it sustains. To Lanie Gerber, this was the key to the future."

"Aha. So, let me ask you: what plans did you and GreenHome have for the Gerbers' hundred-and-thirty-acre golf course in Mashpee?"

For a moment, silence.

"You like to be direct, Detective Altman."

"I'm taking my grandkids to the Ospreys game in an

hour. And I have a short fuse when someone in my community, particularly a healthy woman in the prime of her life, turns up dead."

Carl Hammond's eyes narrowed. "I hope you don't think Harriet Benbow's death was connected in any way to our tribe."

"Mr. Hammond, like I said, I'm just here to gather facts." Altman thumb-flipped his notebook for emphasis. "So far, it looks like that lunch at the Back End was the last time anyone saw Harriet Benbow alive. I'm not trying to connect her death to your tribe, but I need to know what you talked about."

Carl Hammond picked up a chunk of antler and turned it over, as if he hadn't noticed the difference before between its rough and smooth sides.

"That is a simple question," he said, "but I can't give you a simple answer. You may know that Mr. Harrington's invitation came with a pledge of confidentiality. You may know also that the property you mentioned is almost as large as the Mashpee part of our reservation. You call it a golf course. To us it is sacred ground. This is the contradiction that complicates all our dealings with the so-called owners of our ancestral lands." Hammond rolled the stubby cylinder in his fingers, weighing his words. "GreenHome was a family company. Harriet Benbow in some ways stepped into Lanie Gerber's shoes. Yesterday's lunch gave her a chance to speak and to listen." He set down the antler. "Did something that happened there set her feet on a dangerous path? I can't tell you. If I were you, detective, I would ask the Gerbers."

Chapter 9: Play Ball

Instead of following Carl Hammond's advice, Detective Altman followed a hunch.

The crowd in the lobby had thinned out, but he could hear laughter and shouting across the terrazzo floor. Somewhere behind one of those doorways was a tribal gathering place.

He found his purple-haired escort hanging out near the receptionist's desk. "Hey, sorry to trouble you again. I need to see Chief Red Otter?"

"I don't know if he's here." When Altman didn't go away, the kid heaved a philosophical sigh and led him to the door where the noise was loudest. "Yeah," pointing inside. "There."

Not a dining room or cafeteria, but a basketball court. Two teams of pint-sized players in quart-sized uniforms were running up and down the court, while assorted relatives hollered from the bleachers or chatted on the sidelines. The man Detective Altman assumed was Red Otter—burly, late 50s, worn jeans, red plaid flannel shirt, silver-streaked black hair in a braid down his back—stood with one of the coaches. He didn't look like a chief as much as someone's grandpa.

Maybe he *was* someone's grandpa. A small child toddled up and clung to his leg. An older girl of four or five ran over and tugged on his shirt. He scooped up both of them and swung them, shrieking, around in circles.

When they staggered away, Altman stepped in. "Chief

Red Otter? Detective Pete Altman, Exmouth Police."

A deep guttural sound acknowledged the introduction. After a few seconds the chief took the detective's extended hand. "Good game," he rumbled.

"Yeah." The clock showed a score of 25 to 38 with three minutes remaining in the fourth quarter. "Nice place you've got here."

"What do you want, detective?"

"Two things, Chief." A wild shot narrowly missed the coach, who moved toward his team's basket. "I'd like to get back to Quansett and take my grandkids to a baseball game. And since it's my job to investigate the death of Ms. Harriet Benbow of GreenHome LLC, I'd like to hear about your lunch conversation yesterday."

"You talk to Mudge?"

"Briefly."

"Hammond?"

"Yes. Just now."

"Someone killed her?"

"We don't know that for sure. Waiting for the autopsy report. I will tell you it looks unlikely that Ms. Benbow died of natural causes."

The chief half-closed his eyes. "No," he said eventually. "No conversation. For the birds to land, the water must be still. This woman was impatient."

Evidently this was a dismissal, but Pete Altman wasn't finished. "You didn't talk to her at all?"

Red Otter's head moved an inch left and right.

"Because she was impatient?" Pause. "Did that bother anyone else?"

The chief's shoulders rose and fell.

"What plans do the GreenHome folks have for the old golf course they own in Mashpee?"

No reply.

"Chief Red Otter, can I ask— Why did you go to that lunch?"

His eyes opened. "To taste my cousin's cooking."

A fracas erupted on the basketball court. Red Otter strolled over to investigate, or perhaps mediate. Pete Altman took that as permission from Fate to start his overdue afternoon off.

Crossing the lobby, he could picture the chief and the council chair laughing tonight about how they'd baffled the white cop with their cryptic Indian answers. He could also picture them calling a pow-wow, or a lawyer, or forgetting he'd been here the minute he walked out the door.

In his years of playing professional cat-and-mouse, Detective Altman had not dealt with many Wampanoags. Mudge at the Back End, was about it. A few drug incidents, parties that got out of hand, vehicle mishaps—but not up close like this. Not as Persons of Interest in a case he hoped he wouldn't blow by simple cluelessness.

Never mind. He had overcome cluelessness in Iraq, a lot harder than this. He'd do the same here. Follow procedure; take nothing personally. When he was ready to interview Carl Hammond or Red Otter again, Detective Altman would call a tribal police officer. For now, he had an Ospreys game to catch.

He did wonder, though, how many stops he'd have to pull out before someone told him what happened at Tony Harrington's lunch.

➤➤

Lydia and Edgar met at 6 PM in the driveway. To him it was the driveway—for lack of a better word, he said, since one must refer to it somehow. To her it was the grassy patch behind the boxwood hedge where they parked their cars, six yards from Edgar's door. Ten yards below the stone snake he'd laid out on the hillside, which Lydia used as a path up to her cottage. One of her proudest achievements since she'd moved in was learning how to downshift her Morris Minor around the corner of Quansett's town green and through the gap in the hedge without braking.

She found him leaning against his black VW wagon, inking in a New York Times crossword puzzle. Edgar hated being late for anything. Lydia hated being early. Her way of making it up to him for making him wait was to transform herself from kitchen drudge into arm candy. For tonight's dinner date she wore wedge-heeled rainbow sandals, a green sundress which three months ago had matched the streaks in her hair, and two-and-a-half pairs of earrings. Edgar hadn't changed out of his khaki shorts and blue work shirt.

He folded the paper into his pocket, and looked her over with what she hoped was admiration. "Shall we give Sea Fare a try?"

"Absolutely." Lydia had been craving fresh swordfish all summer. The only seafood served at the Back End was canned tuna.

"What news from our friend Detective Altman?"

"Not much." She described their Q&A in the back room.

"I had a call from Leo." Edgar unlocked the car. "Tony's at the police station. They've taken his house keys and confiscated his car."

"How is he?"

"Leo's beside himself. Tony, I can only imagine. But if the police are searching for a weapon, this is a more than suspicious death. What was your sense?"

"Same thing. They don't know much yet, but it doesn't look good. I mean, asking Dinah if she's missing anything at all from the kitchen—a knife, a meat hammer, a spatula, an egg beater?"

"Hummy hummy hoo. And tomorrow is Sunday." They buckled seat belts. "Did I tell you about the new story I've begun fiddling with?"

In Lydia's opinion, having to wait a whole day for more news was no reason to change the subject. "Not yet, but that reminds me. Can we stop by the Frigate? I need to check something with Mudge."

Edgar was such an enthusiastic patron of Quansett's local bookstore that head clerk and tech wizard Wally Hicks had put him on speed-dial. "Oh, sure, why not." With a hand on the gearshift he added, "I hardly dare hope they've got in my Japanese cinema books."

The elegantly restored Frigate filled a tall Victorian building across Main Street from the Back End. Gromit, the shop's resident Labrador retriever, greeted them at the door.

"Hey, Mr. Rowdey." Wally Hicks waved from the front counter. "And Lydia. Welcome."

Gromit's tail flailed against Lydia's leg as Edgar tousled his ears: "Wuzzum wuzzum!" Gromit tried to lick his nose.

"Where's Mudge?" Lydia asked Wally.

"Last seen in Film and Theater."

She made her way back through the Frigate's labyrinthine shelves. Mudge was squatting beside a carton of new arrivals. Hadn't he heard her and Edgar come in?

He glanced up without his usual grin. "Hey."

"Hey. Are you hiding?"

"I'm working."

This wasn't like him. "Mudge, is everything OK?"

"Sure." He stood up. "Long couple of days. What's up? You look like the cat's meow."

Relieved, she pirouetted. "In my cat's pajamas? I can't look like a million bucks, because I'm about to blow my entire yesterday's tip on dinner with Edgar. But I wanted to talk to you about Tony's lunch. Before the cops come sniffing around."

"They already did."

"Again. They took Tony down to the station and they're searching his car. So they must think it's murder, right?"

Mudge shrugged.

"Meaning Detective Altman will come back Monday with pushier questions. Today softballs, tomorrow hand grenades." Lydia rested her elbow on a bookshelf. "Like, why were your cousins at a meeting about SailPort Landing?"

"Like, were you friends with Harriet Benbow?"

"Yeah." Lydia wished Mudge would give her a clear sign that in this, as in all Back End business, they were still allies. "So, what do we say? I mean, OK, the truth, the whole truth, and all that, but I don't want to get into the weeds. Not if they're full of . . ."

"Snakes?"

"I was thinking poison ivy, but yeah."

He bent to pick up a book. "I don't get why you're worrying about it."

"Are you serious?"

"I mean, Tony would have shown Altman that paper, right? So he's pissed, and takes Tony down to the station so Leo won't keep breathing down his neck while he grills him."

"What?" This was not the scene Lydia pictured. "What paper?"

Mudge shelved the book and faced her. "That privacy thing he made us sign."

Her hand went to her mouth. "Holy jello. I totally forgot!"

"So, no worries. Where you going for dinner?"

"No. Mudge. I forgot to sign it! Tony brought it in, with everybody sitting down for lunch, and, remember? You signed it first because you needed to take the muffins out. I was going to do it after the salad dressing. But I forgot."

Mudge's eyebrows went up. "Huh."

"Did he ever come back to pick it up?"

"Donno." He frowned, thinking back. "He must have. I didn't see it again. So . . ."

"Where does that leave me, legally?" Lydia completed.

That drew a wry smile. "You know what Tony'll say. You agreed to sign it. That's like a verbal contract."

"Like, sign it now and it'll still count for yesterday."

"Well, or if he had to hand it over to the cops, he might have signed it for you."

"Maybe he didn't check. The shape he was in."

Mudge nodded slowly. Whatever he'd been preoccupied about when she came in, it was distracting him again.

"If my name's not on that thing, I'm back to Square One," she said. "I don't see Altman buying the retroactive verbal contract idea. But, you know, signed or not, I can't see the cops letting us off the hook in a murder case because we promised not to talk about Tony's real-estate deals. And I also don't see Altman buying that we were too busy feeding everybody to hear anything they said."

Mudge was watching her now. Lydia rallied her courage. "You're right. I met Harriet Benbow in Cambridge. We were not friends. I wasn't happy to see her, and I wanted to know what she was doing here. So when I could, I eavesdropped. And I heard her say GreenHome was reviewing Lanie Gerber's two unfinished projects, and they might change their plans."

For a moment Mudge didn't speak. Then he said, "You can't tell the cops that."

"If they ask me?"

"Say you promised Tony. Let them prove if it's not legally binding."

"What do you think would be a problem with saying

that? Not what the plans are, seeing as I don't know."

"Right. You don't. As far as anybody knows, there's no connection between SailPort Landing and Mashpee. So why would you tell the cops there is? That's all the excuse they need to pin Harriet Benbow's murder on the Indians. The savages who they've been trying to wipe off our land ever since the Mayflower."

"Right now it sounds like they're trying to pin it on Tony."

"Maybe they should."

"You think Tony killed her?"

"Lydia. If GreenHome did change their plans—like, say if they broke their promise to the tribe and tried to build a development on our land—where would that leave Tony?"

She didn't understand his ferocity. "Greasing wheels in Mashpee instead of Quansett?"

"No. Up a creek without a paddle. Tony can't work in Mashpee. The only wheels he can grease are Town of Exmouth. That's Quansett and three other villages. Mashpee's a separate town, with its own rules."

Lydia pondered. Mudge grabbed more books and rammed them into the rows on the shelves, as if he urgently needed to assert control over something.

"Your cousins didn't act upset," she said. "What's his name—Carl? The council chairman? He seemed fine with it. And Red Otter—I never heard him say a word."

Mudge turned on her. "You don't know them. Did you ever see either of them before today? Did you ever talk to them?"

"I might have, at the Pow-Wow in July," said Lydia. "That's the only time I've been to Mashpee."

"Did you go to the other part of town? Around Mashpee Pond? The Wampanoag Museum? What do you know about our history?"

"Hey, take it easy! I've only lived here since June, and I work six days a week." She touched his arm. "Mudge, this is me. Your friend Lydia. Your business partner. That's why I'm here, is to get your advice, so I don't screw this up."

He let out a long sigh. Then he slung his arm around her shoulder. "It's already screwed up. Not your fault. Sorry."

A familiar voice called from the front counter: "Yoo-hoo!"

They both waved to Edgar. Mudge murmured to Lydia: "Time's running out on the Early Bird Specials."

"Yeah. So, listen. I'll stonewall as best I can, OK? But I think things are maybe about to get complicated."

Chapter 10: Sea Fare

According to Edgar, the only visible difference between Sea Fare and the gray-shingled, red-shuttered, white-trimmed restaurant it had replaced was the carved wooden swordfish on the side of the building. He and Lydia were welcomed by a smiling hostess who ushered them to a booth in the bar room. Sorry, no, she couldn't seat them on the porch. For a waterfront table, a reservation was required.

Lydia stifled an impulse to ask if that meant Wampanoags got first dibs.

They ordered gin-and-tonics. "Have you been to the Wampanoag Museum in Mashpee?" she asked Edgar.

"Not in donkey's years." He peered at the menu. "Hmm, really? Scallops scallopini?"

"What's it like?"

"Much as you'd expect. Lemon juice, mushrooms . . . "

"The museum?"

"Oh." Looking up over the rims of his glasses. "Zippy. Worth stopping in sometime when you're out that way."

Their drinks arrived, each topped with a lime wedge skewered on a toothpick arrow. Their waitress introduced herself as Shirley and assured Edgar the scallopini was delicious. The chef used bay scallops, not sea scallops, and breaded them whole. Edgar decided to try it. Lydia ordered swordfish tips.

Stabbing her lime, she asked him, "Have you talked to

Leo again? Any news?"

"Yes and no. Tony balked at signing a police statement without his lawyer, but Fred Jones is gone for the weekend. Leo's hoping Detective Altman will run into him at the Ospreys game and they'll sort it out."

"Is this now officially a murder case?"

"Not yet, according to Leo, but that seems to be a formality."

"Do the cops think Tony killed her?"

"My dear, I didn't ask. However!" He lifted a meaningful eyebrow. "And you?"

"Me, what?"

"You were at that lunch. You've just had a confab with Mudge behind the bookshelves. What do you think?"

Lydia took a large swallow of gin-and-tonic before answering. "I think if I talk about this, I lose my . . . what do you call it? Deniability."

Edgar nodded and surveyed the other tables around them. This was Lydia's first encounter with Early Bird Specials. Until she started working at Leo's, she'd never heard of the drinks-plus-dinner Happy Hour for retirees that was as popular a ritual among Back End customers as church or Bingo. She and Edgar had shown up at the tail end, too late for the second or third half-price cocktail that had some of these white heads nodding over their Indian pudding.

"If you want my opinion," he said, "your deniability is safe here."

"What if I told you something hypothetical," said Lydia, "and the cops questioned you about it. Would you have to report it?"

"Short of a criminal confession, I don't see how."

"OK. First, a question. Suppose the Flying Wedge got a job catering a private business luncheon. And suppose the guy in charge made everybody, including the caterers, sign a nondisclosure agreement. If one of the guests later becomes a crime victim, does that agreement apply to police interviews?"

"Well, you'd want to check with a lawyer. But I very much doubt it."

"Now, suppose, hypothetically, I met the crime victim once. Years ago, before I moved here. When I lived somewhere else under a different name. Suppose she was a therapist, and I had a bunch of stuff to sort out and I got referred to her. I'm not big on therapy, but I go, and she seems like a smart sensible person, so I spill my guts. And while I'm blowing my nose, she says, You were right to come in, too bad you're going through all this, sorry, our time's up. Tell you what. I can try and squeeze you into my weekly crisis support group. It's full, but there should be a slot opening up in a month or two." Lydia paused for a gulp of her drink. "I guess she could see from my face what I thought of that. So she says, Not the answer you wanted, but your insurance doesn't cover individual sessions, and I think you'll resonate with these women. What happened after that I don't exactly remember, except I slammed the door so hard it was like a bomb blast."

"Mm," said Edgar sympathetically.

"So, if the cops ask me if I know this person, do I have to say yes? Since I really don't know her, I just met her that one time. Only for some reason she recognized me at Leo's and came over to ask how I was doing. Which probably somebody saw. Hypothetically."

"Yes. Well, no. You know they say the difficulty is never the crime so much as the cover-up. With regard to other people, I generally feel there's no need to tell the police anything they can find out just as well on their own. But regarding oneself, one doesn't want them finding out anything on their own that they'll claim one should have volunteered. If you follow me."

Their entrees arrived. Lydia took a deep breath. Normally she felt a surge of solidarity with fellow restaurant workers. But given Edgar's willingness to be distracted by almost anything from almost anything, she silently urged Shirley the waitress to put down their plates and go away.

"Fresh pepper?"

"We're fine."

"Everything looks yummy," Edgar added.

"Freshen up those drinks for you?"

"No thanks," Lydia said tightly.

Edgar held up his glass. "Sure, why not?"

As soon as Shirley was out of earshot Lydia said, "You don't think telling the cops I met the deceased would put me on the suspect list?"

"How can that be avoided? From their point of view, everyone at that lunch had means and opportunity. As far as motive, Tony's still way ahead of you. I take it you're concerned about the Wampanoags."

She'd learned early in their acquaintance not to be thrown off balance by Edgar's habit of leapfrogging straight to a conclusion that would take anyone else several zigs and zags. "Yes."

"Hypothetically, may I ask why?"

Lydia chugged the dregs of her gin-and-tonic. "Suppose somebody was found dead who'd just announced that her company might renege on a promise. Say they own a big chunk of land in Mashpee which they planned to turn over to the Wampanoags once their tribal status got resolved. Only a principal in the company died while that was still in limbo. So this new spokeswoman says, Yeah, all settled now, but how many times have we heard that? Here's this other project, waterfront condos in Quansett. Also stuck in red tape. What if they were switched? Build housing on the Mashpee golf course, accommodating the tribe of course, and donate the Quansett salt marsh to a land trust?"

Edgar was frowning—for him, a rare display of emotion. "Indian giver."

"Ha! Bingo, to quote the Early Birds."

They each took a bite. After a moment Edgar inquired: "What does Mudge say?"

"Not much. His two cousins at the lunch didn't, you know, go on the warpath. The chief, Red Otter, didn't react at all. The only time I heard a peep out of him was when they first got there and he said hi to Mudge. The other one, Carl something, he's more of a negotiator. Very cool, like he wanted to suss things out and maybe go back to the tribe before he made a commitment. But did you see Mudge at the Frigate? Hiding behind the bookshelves. When I asked him what was up, he practically yelled at me."

"Hummy hummy hoo," said Edgar thoughtfully.

"Gin and tonic?" came a voice from above.

He looked up. "Thank you, Shirley."

As the waitress showed signs of lingering, Lydia held out her empty glass. "Same here."

When they were alone again, Edgar said, "About my new story."

For a moment Lydia had no idea what he was talking about. Then she remembered putting him off back in the driveway.

"Some friends of mine are starting a magazine. *Golden Age Mysteries.* They've asked several of our old New York crowd to write pastiches for an Agatha Christie tribute issue. Not that film and TV haven't trotted out enough Miss Marples, Hercule Poirots, and so forth to bore the socks off us all. A new twist, is what they requested. However iddy-ottic. Mine is 'The

Toastrack Enigma.'"

He peered at her expectantly over the rim of his glass.

"What, Agatha Christie goes yard-saling?"

His lips pursed: she'd missed the point. She tried again: "So what's the enigma?"

"I'd have mentioned it at Leo's this morning if not for all the hoo-ha. The minute I said yes to the magazine, I thought: Oh dear! My mind is an utter blank. I went out in search of inspiration, and there it was. Art Deco, silver under the tarnish, nearly the same vintage as Dame Agatha herself. And priceless. No price tag. I carried the toastrack up to the lady with the cash box, and she was flummoxed. 'What's that thing doing here?' I said, 'It was sitting by itself on the back table.' She said, 'It can't be. I sold it yesterday.'"

Shirley the waitress brought Lydia's gin-and-tonic. Edgar and Lydia ignored her.

"Well! I said. Perhaps the buyer forgot it. Or changed his mind. Oh no, she said. This was three people who came together, and right away, they all wanted it. Squawking like a bunch of seagulls. *I saw it first! I need it more!* And while two of them are fighting, their friend grabs it out from under their nose. Laughing: 'You snooze, you lose!' She hands me the money, and off they go in their red convertible. One nose in the air and two noses out of joint."

Lydia felt as if a baseball had hit her in the stomach. "In their red— Did you ask . . .?"

"Oh yes. The toastrack-snatcher was a small dark-haired lady in a flowered dress. The other girl, blonde, tennis clothes. The driver she described as a hunk, flirting with both of them."

"Harriet Benbow, Rosalie Gerber, and Tony Harrington."

"Mm." Edgar pushed his glasses up his nose.

Such a swarm of questions filled Lydia's brain that it took her a moment to pick one: "How did the toastrack get from the yard sale to Tony's car back to the yard sale again?"

"I assure you, I haven't a clue."

"It makes no sense."

"No," he agreed.

"Any way you look at it. One, Harriet grabs the toastrack. Two, Tony kills her, drinks himself stupid, realizes she left it in his back seat, and staggers out to the car, but instead of dumping it in the nearest bin, he drives across town to return it to the yard sale? I don't think so. Rosalie fumes through lunch because Harriet stole her toastrack, kills her to get it back, and then drops it off at the yard sale on her way to scatter her mom's ashes at sea? No way."

Edgar sighed.

"It can't be a coincidence. It must mean something, but what?" Lydia spun her lime wedge on its toothpick arrow. "The toastrack wakes up in Tony's Mustang convertible, climbs out, and finds its way home like a lost kitten?"

"You're getting punchy, dear. Have some more gin."

She did.

"One is also tempted to ask," Edgar continued, "Was it the police Tony ran away from, or the toastrack?"

"At Leo's, you mean? Why would he run away from the toastrack?"

"Why does anyone do anything? The point is, Tony didn't leave his post at the register when Officer Kelly came in for coffeecake. And announced a body had been found at SailPort Landing. But when I unwrapped the toastrack, on the counter right next to Tony, he went pale as a ghost. Next thing you know, poof! Disappeared!"

"Tony was already pale as a ghost, Edgar. He had a killer hangover. And between you unwrapping the toastrack and him disappearing, Detective Altman showed up asking questions about his lunch guests."

"Be that as it may." Edgar popped a scallop into his mouth.

"Maybe he knew something we don't." Lydia swirled her drink. "Like, why did he want it so badly he'd fight over it with his own clients?"

"Why indeed."

"Art Deco. Silver. Agatha Christie vintage. Could it be priceless?"

"I hardly think so. Not without a provenance. You know, a rare silversmith's mark, or an undiscovered letter: 'My dear Mrs. Christie, I do hope you'll adore this toastrack as much as I adored *The Murder on the Links*. Yours ever, Louis Tiffany.'"

"*Murder on the Links*." Lydia flicked her arrow's red cellophane feathers. "That's why Mudge doesn't want us to tell the cops about that hint that GreenHome might switch their condo project from Quansett to Mashpee. He thinks they'd jump on it as a murder motive."

"You mean, the Wampanoags killed Harriet Benbow to get their land back?"

She nodded. "Hard to blame them. Before it was golf links it was an ancient burial ground."

"Except, how would that help? I can't imagine Miss Benbow's name is on the deed. And it still begs the toastrack enigma."

"The toastrack enigma. I hope you're not— Oh, crêpes! Edgar!" Lydia dropped her lime. "Where is the toastrack? Did the cops take it?"

"Heavens no. I left it at Leo's, on the mantelpiece. It should be all right there until Monday. I left a message for Detective Altman suggesting he drop by at his earliest."

"We should go get it! Don't you think? Seeing as everybody in Quansett knows where Leo hides the key? I mean, it could be evidence."

He sighed. "I suppose so."

"Anyway, you'll need it for your story, won't you? Your MacGuffin."

"Too true." Picking up his fork, he changed the subject. "How are the swordfish tips?"

"Outstanding. How's the scallopini?"

"Delicious. Enigmatic. More of a scampi, I'd have said. Of course if they'd called it that, I could have resisted."

Lydia raised her glass. "Hypothetically."

Chapter 11: The Ketch

Driving past the *Wooded Waterfront Homes* sign into SailPort Landing, Louise French wished she'd said no. In her business, weekends were crunch time. This one had worn her out and it was only half over. She should be home on her deck uncorking a Chardonnay, not heading back to the condo where she'd found Harriet Benbow's body.

She'd only said yes because how could she say no to Brad Gerber? Someone had remarked on the memorial cruise that Brad looked like roadkill. Can you blame him? Louise returned. Her friendship with the Gerbers was more professional than personal, but she'd never met a tighter couple. Brad's strong-and-silent stoicism fit surprisingly well with Lanie's passion for saving things: injured birds, her waterfront townhomes, the Wampanoags' heritage. When Lanie got sick, Louise wondered how Brad would cope. She'd welcomed Harriet's inquiry last week about listing the Yawl, Ketch, and Sloop—for the business, sure (any Cape realtor would kill to work with GreenHome LLC), but also as a sign Brad was pulling his shattered life back together.

Louise parked her Mercedes behind a burgundy sedan. For once she didn't mind being the last one to show up at an appointment.

Brad's silver SUV filled the driveway. Brad leaned against it, talking with a tall woman in a beige pantsuit. Louise didn't recognize her: thin but strong-looking, coral lipstick, a long angular nose, short bouffant strawberry-blonde hair. Good lord, surely he hadn't already hired a new assistant?

"Louise." He clasped her hand. "You know State Police Detective Adrienne Hall?"

Detective Hall led them up the walk. "Detective Altman and I want to thank both of you for helping us out." Her not-quite Southern twang made Louise wonder what she was doing in Quansett. "I know it's been a rough day, and you've got a lot on your plates."

A uniformed officer was removing crime-scene tape from the front door. "Let me reassure you, the Exmouth Police team came in right away to take fingerprints and such," said Detective Hall. "So you don't need to worry about touching anything, or seeing anything upsetting."

Brad Gerber had told Louise that on the phone. Still, she was glad to hear it now, standing on the doorstep where the welcome mat used to be.

"What we're looking for is clues to what happened here last night. You two know this place, right? Layout, security measures, et cetera. Also, very important, you knew Harriet Benbow. We didn't. So, think about this for me. If this was a burglary gone wrong, how did they get in? First into SailPort Landing, and then into this unit. Pick a lock? Jimmy a window? And then, what were they after? Do you notice anything missing, or that wasn't here before? Mrs. French, let's start with you. Step by step, tell me everything you can remember from this morning."

Louise stared at the shiny brass sailboat-shaped door knocker. As she began repeating what she'd told Pete Altman, Detective Hall interrupted. "You heard the bell ring but nobody answered. Did you knock? Did you try the doorknob?"

Louise closed her eyes, struggling to recall. The sequence was automatic: punch in the lockbox code, take out the key, unlock the door. Was that what she'd done?

Now that she thought about it, she wasn't sure. She'd been distracted by smudges of mud on the mat and the front stoop. Her mind was on paper towels when she crossed the threshold, blinking in the glare of sun through the windows, and almost stumbled over the obstacle in the hall.

"OK." Detective Hall opened the door.

The late afternoon sun burnished the bamboo floor to gold. Stepping inside, Louise stopped short. White tape outlined where Harriet Benbow's body had lain.

Her fists clenched against her chest. How on earth—? There'd been so much blood! But of course the police would have cleaners. Good ones, apparently. The floor looked perfect. Louise moved closer: GreenHome would save a lot of time and money if—

Stop. We're not here about real estate.

"Is that as close as you went?" Detective Hall stood a few yards behind her.

Louise took a step back. "Here, I'd say."

"And the blood ended where?"

"I'm not sure. Over there," she pointed.

"You got some on your shoes."

"It was scattered. Smeared around. There must have been spots I didn't notice."

"You're right about that. Those smudges on the Welcome mat? Weren't mud."

Brad Gerber, moving forward, spoke sharply. "So the attacker came in and out by the front door. Is that what you're saying?"

"No sir. It's early days yet. We don't have enough evidence to say much of anything for sure. That's why we're here, is to find out."

Louise French turned. Two officers slipped behind Brad

and headed down the basement stairs. Like cats, she thought, pussyfooting around a big dog. Brad didn't notice. He stood gazing in every direction as if this was all new to him. Which it probably was, since the stagers only finished up last week.

They'd done a nice job. Understatement, that was the key: showcase the location, not the trappings. Whether you paused in the hall, or moved left into the living room with its floor-to-ceiling stone fireplace, or circled around the island into the dining area and kitchen, you were surrounded by windows. At this hour the vivid green panorama of trees and marsh grass was splashed with red and gold, blazing between the azure sky and a neon-blue finger of Cape Cod Bay.

"What the land was meant for." Brad Gerber's voice shook. "Lanie's words. Half her life she worked and waited for this."

"And she succeeded," Louise said. "The first phase of her dream come true." She spoke to Detective Hall. "You've seen the drawings? We're in the Ketch. The other two models are the Yawl and the Sloop. Each with a private deck and views of the salt marsh."

"Named after boats," said the detective. "Where does that come in?"

"Hah!" Brad said. "Good question. We wanted docks and launch facilities so residents could access their homes from the water. Lanie had it all mapped out. But the town kept moving the goalposts."

"Changing their environmental regulations," Louise explained.

"We shrank it down to one dock and boat ramp attached to the clubhouse. Then some bicycle coalition sued to block our fence and our extension of Harbor Lane. Claimed we were impeding an Ancient Way. Meaning an old deer path that's been taken over by dirt bikers. This is the kind of thing Harriet thought Tony Harrington could help with. I can't even tell you how long they ran us around in circles."

"Many months," put in Louise.

"Anyhow, we redesigned the fence to accommodate the wildlife, and we moved the Ancient Way to the other side of the creek where it could be widened and paved to meet the latest accessibility requirements, and linked to the main road by an antique wooden footbridge. No sooner we'd settled that, the Army Corps of Engineers jumped on us about the wetlands setback. Harriet was a champ. She got our three model town-homes grandfathered in, but the rest is on hold." Brad Gerber's eyes shifted from the windows to the outline on the floor. "If you're looking for somebody who wanted Harriet Benbow out of their way? That's where you should start."

Detective Hall shepherded him and Louise French toward the living room. "Ms. Benbow lived in Cambridge, have I got that straight? And commuted to your office in Sandwich?"

Brad nodded. "Three days a week originally. More since my wife died. A couple of times lately she spent the night on Cape."

"Always at SailPort Landing?"

"No. Never. She had a motel she liked in Sandwich. We offered her our guest room, but Quansett's an additional half hour drive each way. And Harriet didn't like the optics. This weekend, all of us here for Lanie's memorial, she decided to give the Ketch a dry run."

"Optics." Detective Hall walked to the windows and leaned to look out. "Your CCTV covers what exactly?"

"Front gate and perimeter fence. Twenty-four seven."

"And the gate is automatic? Run by a cell-phone app?"

"Right. Using license-plate recognition." Brad Gerber settled into the leather armchair next to the fireplace. "With the project in limbo, there wasn't enough traffic to need a guard."

"Several of my clients use this system," said Louise, sitting on the sofa. "I recommended it to Brad, and Harriet set it up."

"It was on her phone," Brad said. "Since that was stolen, our security firm put a temporary in-and-out list on my phone. I told your colleague, Detective Altman, they've been asked to cooperate fully with the police."

"Good. We'll need to check comings and goings."

"Detective Hall, I have a question." His hands clasped his knee. "How did Harriet die? Early days, I get that, but this is—" A little shake of his head tried to convey what he couldn't say in words. "Is it true she was murdered?"

"Mr. Gerber, I wish I could tell you. Like I said on the phone, we're waiting on the medical examiner. Right now all I can say is what you've already heard. It does not appear likely that Ms. Benbow died of natural causes."

The detective gave him a moment. Then she asked them both, "Can you think of anyone who might have wanted to harm her?"

"No."

"You mentioned Ms. Benbow rubbed some folks the wrong way. Any blowback from that? Any recent arguments? Threats?"

"No. I can't see— Harriet was a fine person. Best negotiator I've ever seen. She'd been a therapist before she joined GreenHome. You can ask my daughter. It was Rosalie's idea to ask Harriet for help when Lanie learned her cancer had come back. I don't know how we'd have managed without her. I'm not saying everybody loved her. She was too sharp for that. But nobody fought with her, or threatened her. She gave them no reason."

Louise French looked from the trees outside the living

room to the salt marsh outside the kitchen. She didn't care to meet anyone's eyes right now. *Listen to Brad,* she silently advised the detective. *You want to know about Harriet Benbow? Ask his daughter.*

➥

Upstairs they started in the master bathroom. On any other day Louise would have called Brad's attention to the parchment accordion blind on the skylight above the claw-foot tub, the cotton-puff towels reflected in the marble-tile walls and floors. Today there was no point. No, he told Detective Hall, hardly glancing at the items she showed him. I can't tell you if that's Harriet Benbow's toothbrush or cosmetics bag by the sink, or her green silk robe on the door hook.

For Louise the master bedroom was the Ketch's knock-out feature. Here the whole view was salt marsh. The skylight glowed like a bright canopy over the king-size bed. Snuggled under that quilt at night, peeking through the eight-foot wall of windows, you'd feel as if you were floating on a sea of stars.

The bedside table was homelier: reading glasses, a half bottle of water, a box of tissues. A small suitcase on top of the dresser held underclothes and a bathing suit. Detective Hall slid open a mirrored closet door. Two dresses, a linen jacket with matching slacks, and two T-shirts hung from the rod. Sandals, heels, and running shoes were paired on the floor.

"Do you recognize these as Harriet Benbow's belongings, Mr. Gerber?"

"She wore that dress yesterday." He blew his nose. "I've seen her in the beige outfit. Where's her jewelry?"

"The only jewelry we've found was the gold studs in her ears. What else are we looking for?"

"Her watch. Gold, a lady's Rolex. And a ring. She wouldn't have been wearing it. A velvet box. In her purse? Or her suitcase? Can I . . .?"

"Sure. Go ahead. What kind of ring?"

Brad Gerber answered as he rummaged. "An emerald with two diamonds on a gold band."

Louise French let out a small gasp. "Lanie's ring?"

"Yes." Stoically he faced her and Detective Hall. "Harriet Benbow was going to be my wife."

Chapter 12: Contrasts

Lydia Vivaldi and Edgar Rowdey struck most people who knew them, including themselves, as a strange pair. Even the tastes they shared didn't match. For instance, reading dessert menus. What with the Back End squeezing every item onto a small square of colored paper taped to the wall, Lydia favored lavish descriptions: *Hand-churned Madagascar vanilla ice cream drenched in a lush double-fudge ganache sauce.* Edgar favored the simple but ambiguous: *Custard with seasonal berries.*

Sea Fare's offerings for Early Birds disappointed them both.

Edgar was airing his complaints when Lydia's phone rang.

"Only in a geographic sense, if that. Indian pudding has nothing to do with the Wampanoags and everything to do with the English sweet tooth."

"I'll just see who this is, OK?"

"Not to underrate the Pilgrims' ingenuity. Poor bunnies! Desperate for tea-cakes, and not a teaspoon of sugar or wheat flour for thousands of miles. Just molasses and Indian flour—cornmeal to us—"

"It's Leo." A shiver ran through her. "Do you mind if I . . .?"

"By all means. Though I do feel they ran amok with molasses. Baked beans? Boston brown bread?"

"Hey. Leo. Where are you? How's Tony?"

Edgar fell silent. Lydia said "He's right here." Then, to Edgar: "Tony's sprung. Leo wants to talk to you."

A tinny voice blatted as she passed her phone across the table: "Tell the old codger to buy himself a phone!"

"You guys duke it out." Lydia rose. "I'll be back."

When she returned from the restroom, Edgar was still listening and frowning. "A what?" Another pause. "Merciful heavens. Well, best wishes. I hope to see you both on Monday."

With a grimace, he handed the phone back to Lydia.

"Home free?" she asked.

"I wouldn't say that. The autopsy report's been delayed. Someone told Leo the medical examiner's bogged down with a drug fracas in Hyannis. And of course it's the weekend. The police won't release Tony's car, but they let Leo take him home, with the usual dire warnings not to leave town."

"So she definitely was murdered."

"Oh yes. Unless my ears deceive me, Miss Benbow was scalped."

Lydia goggled. "Scalped?"

"If we're to believe what Leo heard."

"Like, the top of her head cut off? Hair and all?"

"He didn't supply particulars. Needless to remark."

"Cripes! Edgar, that's horrible."

"Mm."

"Why do the cops think Tony would scalp Harriet Benbow?"

"According to Leo, no reason at all. Circumstantial evidence. His exact words were more colorful."

"Circumstantial evidence, like Tony ran out the back door when Detective Altman came in the front? Or like Harriet Benbow rode in his convertible, stole his toastrack, ate his lunch, and then spiked his SailPort Landing deal?"

"Oh, it's a bit worse than that. They found traces of blood in his car. On the pedals and the driver's side mat. And his shoes, although they'd been cleaned. Tony claims to have no idea how it got there. That's why they wanted to search his condo."

"Harriet Benbow's blood?"

"They're checking. They're also searching her townhouse at SailPort Landing. You remember that picturesque lady from Texas?"

"Adrienne Hall? The state police detective? If she's on the case—"

"She's not, according to Leo. Not officially. Or not yet. He said the story is she dropped in to lend a hand on Altman's night off. Leo's not convinced. He's worried she wants to frame Tony because she, that is to say the Commonwealth of Massachusetts, can't go after anyone on Wampanoag territory."

"He can't think Mudge's cousins killed Harriet Benbow! Does he?"

Edgar's eyebrows went up and his eyes went down. Shirley the waitress was approaching, all smiles.

"And what can I get you two for dessert?"

"Brownie and ice cream," Lydia said tersely.

"I'll try your grapenut pudding," said Edgar.

"Coffee?"

"Decaf."

"Make that two."

"Okey-dokey," said Shirley, collecting their dessert menus. "That's two decaf—"

Lydia cut in: "We trust you."

Unruffled, Shirley strolled away. Lydia said, "OK. So this is a mess, right? Nothing adds up. Coming back to Leo's circumstantial evidence. If that is Harriet Benbow's blood on Tony's shoes, then the cops can place him at the scene of the crime. Which he lied about, so, not good. But that only means he put his foot in it. Right? They don't have a murder weapon or any witnesses or motive or anything else to say he killed her."

"Well, exactly. He could have walked in seconds after the poor lady surprised a burglar."

"Who broke into a model home to steal what, though? Her wallet? Her rented dishtowels? The toastrack she'd grabbed away from her friends at a yard sale?"

"More to the point," said Edgar, "what would a burglar want with Harriet Benbow's scalp?"

➤→

Twelve minutes to seven. No customers in the shop, no cars in the Frigate's parking lot. Closing time!

Reaching up to lower the blind and flip the sign on the front door, Mudge jumped as a hand rapped on the glass.

"Am I too late?" mouthed Rosalie Gerber.

Yes! he wanted to say. *Go home!*

He opened the door wide enough to speak. "Sorry, we're closing."

"I rode like a bat out of hell." She leaned her bike against the wall and wiped her forehead on her sleeve. "There's seventeen people in my house! Sitting around my living room drinking and crying and telling stories about my mom. I love them all to pieces, but one more minute, swear to God, I'd have killed somebody."

She slithered out of her Spandex jacket as if she were shedding a skin. She looked younger in her blue and gray workout clothes than she had in tennis whites at Leo's yesterday. Not much older than Lydia.

A late shaft of sunlight turned Rosalie's corn-silk hair to copper. Her shoulders went back; her chin tipped up. She drew in a long deep breath.

Mudge inhaled fresh-cut grass and dinner charcoal-grilling on a barbecue, and stepped outside to join her.

"Nice Airstream." She pointed at the silver blimp parked behind the building. "Yours?"

"Nah. Wally Hicks, head clerk. You know Pirandello? Codcast-dot-net?"

"My God. Pirandello with the webcams? That comes from here?" Rosalie's Nikes crunched on the crushed-clamshell driveway as she craned back to look up at the Frigate's cupola, nestled in the treetops like a giant Victorian birdhouse. "Can I see?"

"Not tonight." Wally and Gromit had set out on their evening stroll to The Whistling Pig for a beer and a biscuit. "Did you want a book? I have to get out of here."

"That's what I told everybody. I need a book! Meaning, I have to get out of here. Since you ask, what I really and truly need? is muffins. Seventeen mouths to feed! Now that I'm here it sounds nuts. But honestly, I adored your cranberry-corn muffins, and I wondered, if you weren't too swamped, if there's any chance you could make some for our brunch tomorrow?"

Mudge smiled and shook his head.

"Huge bribe?"

"Sorry."

"Yeah. Well. It's been that kind of a day." Again Rosalie took in air. This time it came out in a sigh. "You know we scattered my mom's ashes at sea this afternoon."

"Yeah. I'm sorry." A ghostly memory of his own mother tapped on Mudge's heart. He shooed it away. The last thing he needed right now was to get into—what did people like Rosalie call it? Sharing.

"She'd have turned sixty yesterday." Following him into the bookstore. "We took the boat out on the weekend, so the off-Capers could come, but we had our own ceremony on her birthday. She wanted my dad and me to sprinkle one scoop of her ashes in her garden at sunrise. To help the roses grow, so she'd always be close to us." Rosalie gazed at the cards on the revolving rack. "Five-thirty AM. Just me, Dad, and Harriet. I read a poem I wrote for her." She turned abruptly toward Mudge. "Harriet brought pizza. Can you believe? My mom's favorite breakfast. Cold pizza! That's the kind of person Harriet was. And the next day she was dead."

Mudge shook his head sympathetically.

"Sorry. You don't want to hear about this."

You got that right, he thought.

"My dad should be home now from SailPort Landing. He had to go let in the cops. Just for half an hour, the detective said."

"Detective Altman?" Mudge rested his elbows on the counter beside the cash register.

"No, some woman. Kind of a twangy Southern accent?" Rosalie moved restlessly around the Frigate's little lobby. "So I decided the guests could survive ten minutes without me, and I'm halfway out the door when my cell phone rings. Surprise! Tony Harrington."

She said it so sardonically that Mudge wondered if he'd missed something.

"If he's a friend of yours, I'm sorry, but it's no secret. Tony's been lobbying to hook up with GreenHome for years. Flirting with me, flirting with my mom— After she died, he saw where the wind was blowing, and he put the moves on Harriet. I'm not saying she fell for it, but, you know? Why not? He's an attractive guy. She's an attractive woman. If she wanted to spend a couple nights in a model condo at SailPort Landing, what's wrong with that?"

Mudge twisted one shoulder and wished Rosalie would realize this was none of his business.

"So, with Harriet out of the picture, it was like, When's the other shoe going to drop? But, turns out, that's not why he called." She stopped and turned. "Tony was at the police station, and he heard something he wasn't supposed to."

Mudge straightened up. Uneasiness prickled the back of his neck.

"Harriet was scalped."

He stared at her: pale skin sun-reddened and freckled, pale hair wind-tangled, pale blue eyes narrowed as if to peer into his soul.

"I thought you'd want to know."

Why? he wanted to ask her.

"Scalped?" he asked her. "What does that mean?"

"How would I know? Tony didn't get the gory details. All he heard was, the crew that took away her body said there was like, nothing left on the top of her head. And a whole lot of blood."

Mudge couldn't speak. He felt as if he were standing alone in the path of an oncoming steamroller that was headed straight for his tribe.

Why did you bike all the way from the other end of Quansett to tell me this?

Rosalie was wriggling something out of her jacket: a silver flask. She uncapped it, drank, and held it out to Mudge. After three seconds he took it.

"Tony was right," she said. "Even though it's gruesome, I'd rather know. It was driving me crazy that my best friend was dead and the cops wouldn't tell me a damn thing." Tears welled up in her eyes. "I begged our police escort on the boat. Did she have a heart attack, or an accident? Did somebody break in and kill her? What?"

Brandy. Mudge's eyes watered.

"Sorry! No answers till we get the autopsy report!"

"So, did they let Tony go?" His throat stung. "Is he still a suspect?"

"They had to let him go. How can he be a suspect when they won't admit Harriet was murdered? What do they think, she tripped and cut off her own scalp?" Rosalie took another swig. "Or is it more like, this isn't the kind of crime a nice middle-aged white guy like Tony Harrington would commit?"

She offered the flask to Mudge. This time he didn't hesitate.

"You need to close the store," she said. "I'll wait outside."

Usually when he was this bone-tired Mudge clicked into automatic, letting his body check off tasks without bothering his brain. Tonight his brain wouldn't shut up. What did she want from him, this rich middle-aged white lady? Not just muffins. Not just a break from her guests.

He should tell her: *Go home, Rosalie. You don't belong here. Take your problems and your brandy and your bad news somewhere else.*

Except . . . Her crack about Tony lobbying to hook up with GreenHome? It wasn't just Tony. Why else would Chief Red Otter and Tribal Council Chairman Carl Hammond accept a lunch invitation to Leo's Back End? Keeping on friendly terms with the Gerbers was practically in their job description.

For the Wampanoags, land wasn't about business deals, it was about identity. Lanie and Brad and Rosalie had claimed they got that. As soon as the courts resolved the tribe's legal standing, GreenHome would deed over the burial ground to its true owners. This time, for once, the government would not screw the Indians.

That was before Tony's lunch.

Harriet Benbow hadn't exactly U-turned. She'd waffled: *Unexpected challenges. A time of change. Long history. New opportunities. Everything on the table.* Knowing damn well—as

Mudge knew, and Rosalie must, too—what message she was sending.

A message the cops wouldn't need to decode from tom-toms or smoke signals when they started tagging suspects for her murder.

As a chief's son, Mudge had learned since childhood about balancing loyalty and diplomacy. *Don't listen to what they say, listen to what they do.* Was Harriet Benbow opening a discussion, as she claimed, or announcing a change of plans? Why did Rosalie Gerber show up here tonight? These were not his questions to answer. His question was how to keep the balance.

Mudge set the Frigate's alarm system. He didn't see Rosalie outside the window. Could she have eavesdropped on his thoughts and left? No, her bike was still leaning against the wall.

Ah, there she was. An extra silhouette on the boulder up by the streetlamp. Lit by the only firefly in this late Indian-summer season, her silver flask.

He turned off the lights and went out to join her.

Chapter 13: Incoming

On the other side of Exmouth, State Police Detective Adrienne Hall sat reading Officer Ricky Hanlon's report on the Gerbers' ash-scattering ceremony. She didn't mind working on a Saturday night. Things tended to get so crazy downstairs, the incoming flood from parties, accidents, fights, and whatnot, that nobody cared if you squirreled yourself away upstairs in Pete Altman's empty office. Nobody noticed if you hadn't done your hair or put on makeup. You could kick off your shoes, leave the lid off your coffee, and hear yourself think.

The quiet made it easier to translate official prose into a 3-D picture. Officer Hanlon's report drew a sketch of what had happened aboard the schooner Calliope. Perspective and color would come from interviews tomorrow with the Gerbers' guests. In Hanlon's version, the most colorful character was (ironically) Rosalie Gerber, storming around like a black silk thundercloud.

Adrienne Hall herself had expanded the case file quite a bit in the forty minutes she'd just spent with Rosalie's dad. For that she owed big thanks to Louise French, bless her sharp realtor's instincts. Or woman's instincts. How much effort had it taken Ms. French not to flinch when Brad Gerber dropped his bombshell? Her perfect smile hadn't budged as she sized up the situation, offered her condolences, and excused herself so Detective Hall could continue this conversation one-to-one.

Hall's cell phone buzzed. "Hey, Pete."

"Hey, Adrienne. I got your message. Any news on the autopsy?"

"Still working on exact cause of death. I got a tentative window for the attack, though. Seven to ten PM."

"Huh."

"Yeah. Kind of early for a B and E."

"Did Ricky Hanlon pick up anything on the yacht?"

"No surprises. He thinks he might have better luck on land tomorrow interviewing the Gerbers' guests. You know, though, Pete, we're digging for gold in a copper mine over there."

"Eliminating suspects," Altman reminded her. "Narrowing the field."

"Got to be done," Hall agreed. "Narrow it down from anyone involved with GreenHome LLC, the Mashpee Wampanoag tribe, and who am I leaving out?"

"Leo Harrington's customers and staff at the Back End. What's that, a thousand or so total?But look on the bright side. GreenHome's CCTV has ruled out a vagrant burglar climbing over the SailPort Landing fence."

"Well now, I sure am relieved to hear that, detective. Hey, how'd your baseball team do?"

"Ospreys won! Turned it around from three-zero to six-three in the eighth inning. Terrific game."

She could picture his grin under that sheepdog hair. "Your grandkids must've been thrilled."

"Them and me both. Now, can we cut to the chase, detective?"

"You want to pop a beer first? Because this is the not-so-bright side coming up."

Over the distant shrieks of children, Adrienne Hall heard

a deep sigh on the other end of the phone.

"How'd our perp get in?" she resumed. "Not over the fence. Good. Now, here's what I found out from Brad Gerber and Louise French. With nobody living at SailPort Landing, they installed an automatic gate. Works by license-plate recognition, run by an app on Harriet Benbow's phone. So whoever took that phone—for the sake of argument, let's say her killer —also took the time-and-date records of who's been in and out, and the list of authorized plates."

"Damn!"

"Amen. The security company's working on it, but don't hold your breath. For now we have a best-I-can-recall list from Gerber and French, and that shoots us right back to Tony Harrington. Last night, between his lunch and her murder, Harriet Benbow told Brad the current list had fifteen plates on it, including Tony's Mustang convertible."

"What about the other fourteen?"

"Well now, the gate was Harriet's baby, and Brad said he could only guess. Him and Rosalie and Harriet, obviously. GreenHome's contractor, James Hardy. Louise French said two of the authorized plates are hers, a company car and her Mercedes. The others, her best guess is the plumber, the landscaper, the Town of Exmouth meter reader, the police beat cop, and the fire department's main engine and ambulance. And, the kicker? Mario's Mexican and Pizza."

There was a half minute of silence.

"Mrs. French tells me they make quite a tasty pie," Hall added.

"Don't stop there," said Altman.

"When the cleaners were in on Tuesday, they found a delivery receipt on the deck. Mrs. French checked with Mario, and he confirmed Harriet Benbow placed an order last week.

So I gave him a call, and whaddya know? Mario's delivered a large spinach, mushroom, and garlic to Two Harbor Lane at 8 PM Thursday night."

"The night before she died."

"Yep."

"Why large?"

"To share with a friend? For leftovers in case Tony's lunch on Friday went south?"

"So what do you think, Adrienne? Was this a regular thing with her? Staying in an empty model townhouse? Without telling anybody but the pizza guy?"

"You got me," said Hall. "A picnic on the deck, I can see that. Spending the night, not without a sleeping bag. The staging company only finished spiffing the place up last week." She grinned into the phone. "But since you ask. . . ."

When she told him about the engagement between Harriet Benbow and Brad Gerber, Altman's silence lasted for so long that Hall lifted her foot onto his desk. She'd stubbed her toe checking the Ketch's sliding doors. It had stopped throbbing but still looked puffy. In the circumstances, she didn't think Pete would mind.

His first question was the same one she'd have asked. "You think Gerber was telling the truth?"

"If he wasn't, he oughta be in pictures. Hard to verify, though, with the ring gone missing."

"And her phone," Altman said.

"No diary found among her belongings," Hall affirmed. "No photo in his wallet. No smoochie texts or emails. Neither one of them was big on social media, but we can start snooping around tomorrow for breadcrumbs."

"Who else knew about this?"

"Not a soul." She inspected the scrape alongside her

toenail. "Louise French was politely staggered, and she's known him for ages. "

"Not even Rosalie?"

"Least of all Rosalie. Not because she'd've objected. Just the opposite. They thought she'd be so tickled she'd let the cat out of the bag, and upset the folks who'd come to honor her mama."

Pete thought that over. "Lanie Gerber died when?"

"Six months ago. Friday would have been her sixtieth birthday."

"And Brad popped the question to Harriet when?"

"Friday afternoon." Adrienne wiggled her toe like a joystick, back and forth, side to side. "The way he tells it, he dropped by the townhouse after lunch to tell her he didn't like how Tony Harrington was flirting with her. She said, that's show biz, and what's it to you? Next thing he knows, he's handing her Lanie's emerald ring."

"Whoa!"

"And not only did she say yes instead of telling him where to shove it. She insisted on that very ring."

"Hold on. Harriet wanted Brad to give her the same engagement ring that his first wife, her ex-boss, wore for thirty-plus years of marriage?"

"That's what he says. It's a family heirloom, passed down like a coat of arms. Out of respect for the memorial, they agreed Harriet wouldn't wear it until the guests went home and they could ask Rosalie for her blessing, and the three of them could make the announcement together."

"Well, blow me down with a dog whistle. What do you think? Do you believe it?"

Not broken, Hall decided, just bruised. "I think he believes it."

"And here I was looking forward to sitting down with Mr. Gerber tomorrow and getting some straight answers on this case."

"I hear ya," she said. "Not even officially a homicide yet, and between the Harringtons, the Wampanoags, and the Gerbers, we're barking up more trees than Smokey the Bear."

"That's our problem," said Altman. "Too many trees and no forest."

"One foot in front of the other. Best we can do."

After a moment he asked, "You still see Tony as the front runner?"

"Speaking of feet? No results from the lab, Pete. I'd have told you."

"Sure."

"Maybe he'll get lucky. Maybe somebody out there is turning in Harriet Benbow's wallet as we speak, or fencing her jewelry, or finding the weapon that killed her. But as of right now, Tony Harrington is the guy who claims he never saw his guest of honor again after lunch yesterday, and hasn't got a clue why there's blood in his car and on his shoes, which if you believe in the laws of probability is most likely a match for hers and the footprints at the scene."

Pete Altman didn't answer for a moment. Then he said, "I can't argue with any of that."

"But?"

"But why the heck would he steal her toupée?"

Adrienne Hall slipped into her shoes. "You got me there, detective."

➤➤

So where are the Wampanoags?
Lydia didn't expect the Town of Mashpee to welcome

visitors with a carved wooden arch, like Disneyland, or even a sign. But all she'd seen for the last few miles was trees.

WiFi on the Cape was notoriously spotty. Did they ration it on Sundays, like liquor sales? As a sovereign nation, did the tribe have its own network? Maybe a break in her GPS had sent her and her yellow Morris Minor past a key turn. It just didn't make sense that the route from Exmouth to Mashpee would be called South Sandwich Road.

She passed a pair of driveways with mailboxes but no address.

Where the hell am I?

Where is Mashpee?

Where are the Wampanoags?

South Sandwich Road spilled her onto Main Street. The trees thinned. Lydia's hopes rose and then fell. White-trimmed gray clapboard buildings, a dance studio, a coffee shop, clusters of almost-new Cape Cod houses . . . This couldn't be right.

It must be, though. At a traffic light she spotted signs: Mashpee Country Store. Mashpee Community Park. Still nothing that looked . . . Well, OK. Face it: she had no idea if 21st-century New England Indians lived in wigwams or trailers or faux-Colonial cottages. Mudge she knew shared a house with his dad and his sister Summer Moon and their younger half-siblings, except when his dad's girlfriend pitched a meltdown and Mudge camped under the giant beech tree behind Leo's frog pond.

She'd meant to call him. Then she thought she'd stop by The Frigate, where he often worked on Sundays. But she didn't see his truck in the parking lot; and, face it, she really didn't want to be the person who told him Harriet Benbow had been scalped. His edginess last night had shaken her. In the few months since Lydia arrived on Cape Cod—from her point of view, perched here like a bird on a twig—their comradeship at the Back End and their partnership in the Flying Wedge had become cornerstones of her life. Last night she'd felt Mudge pulling back. Because he didn't trust her, a wash-ashore ten years older than he was, to understand where he was coming from? That wasn't a gap she could bridge with words. Better to take his advice and educate herself.

The wooden sign for the Mashpee Wampanoag Indian Museum marked a steep driveway. Next to it stood an antique half-Cape house, aproned by a small flower garden and a neat lawn. Lydia parked in the lot at the bottom of the hill. Only two other cars—not many visitors for a Sunday afternoon.

Across from her, at the edge of the woods, some tourist types were stooping to enter a structure roughly the same size and shape as Frigate clerk Wally Hicks's Airstream trailer. Its curved sides were slabs of sun-bleached tree bark, held in place by long slender branches.

To her this odd structure looked as exotic as a space ship. To Mudge it must be as familiar as the gray-shingled buildings she'd passed on her way here.

She wished she'd asked him where he lived. Nearby? His younger brothers and sisters went to school in Mashpee. Half-siblings . . . or were *brother* and *sister* flexible terms here, like *cousin?* Summer, his full sister, took courses at Cape Cod Community College and worked part-time for the tribe. They'd lost their mom to cancer when they were small—the reason Lincoln Miles had abdicated as the tribe's chief. Lydia hadn't met him, but she'd recognized him at the Pow-Wow: tall, strikingly handsome, charming and easygoing, like his son.

And his daughter. Lydia had hoped Summer would be leading museum tours today, and there she was. She looked more Native American than when she'd stopped by Leo's: a plain buckskin-colored dress instead of a hoodie and jeans, long black hair braided with colored beads, a purple-and-white shell necklace. She was shepherding a straggler into the hut. Lydia walked over, waving.

Summer held up a hand and shook her head.

They intersected a few yards from the bark-covered blimp. "We're closed on weekends," Summer said. "This is a private party. Sorry."

No sign of recognition. Lydia reintroduced herself.

"Oh, right. From the Back End." *Your brother's friend and partner in the Flying Wedge,* Lydia felt like reminding her.

"The only reason I'm here is, Congressman O'Keefe is on Cape for the weekend and he really wanted to see our museum."

Behind her, a familiar-looking man in a green polo shirt, khakis, and a Red Sox baseball cap walked toward them, sunburned and smiling. Summer saw Lydia smile back at him and turned.

"How you doing?"

"Congressman, this is Lydia Vivaldi. She works with my brother."

"One of your constituents. Pleased to meet you." Lydia shook his hand, glad that she'd worn her best shorts and a non-political T-shirt. "Sorry, I didn't realize the museum was closed. My one day off."

Congressman O'Keefe flashed his perfect white teeth. "Why don't you join us?"

Chapter 14: Reservations

For his tour of the Mashpee Wampanoag Indian Museum, the congressman had brought along nine family members and friends and a wiry fiftyish man with a high-end Nikon. The photographer stood by the doorway shooting his boss's arrival with his Indian guide. Everyone else was nosing around inside the wooden igloo.

In the center of the dirt floor, an oval of stones outlined a fire pit. A pair of forked branches supported a sapling which appeared to double as a roasting spit and a rod to hang cooking pots. An open smoke-hole in the roof overhead let in light. The hut was unexpectedly bright, thanks partly to white curtains lining the bark walls.

Slender wooden pillars held everything in place, including a wide shelf around the perimeter. To sleep on? Sit on? Eat on? The three kids were testing all the possibilities. The platform rested on a framework of tied-together branches, which didn't look all that sturdy to Lydia. The flat top was covered with animal hides, ranging in size from rabbit to deer. Summer climbed onto it and motioned the others to join her.

"This house is called a wetu. The whole village would live up here in the winter, all close together. You can see how the layers of bark hold in the heat and keep out the rain and snow. In the summer everybody moves closer to the water, more open and spread out."

She continued explaining, pointing, demonstrating. Lydia was too distracted by Summer's resemblance to Mudge, and her matter-of-fact manner, to stay focused. She described the Wampanoags' customs as if this was how people lived now. Listening to her, you almost expected to see more wetus (Wee Twos? We Toos?) scattered through these woods. You could almost believe that the European immigrants who'd paved the roads and built the cars were just a bad dream, a cautionary tale for children.

The group moved outside. In daylight Lydia tagged them as the congressman's wife and daughter, his brother and sister-in-law (the parents of the other two children), Mrs. O'Keefe's parents, and a couple who must be their local hosts. The two girls looked around eleven and the boy maybe seven.

Summer led them to a garden patch, mostly dead now.

"This is how we cultivate our crops—corn, beans, and squash planted together, not in separate fields like the settlers'. Our ancestors learned this over centuries. As the corn sprouts grow into cornstalks, the bean vines twine up around them for support. The squash vines spread out low to the ground, shading the roots and keeping in moisture. The beans add nitrogen to the soil to nourish the corn and squash. All three crops attract insects which eat pests that might harm the plants. And together, beans, squash, and corn provide a healthy, varied diet for our people."

"What about, like, meat?" asked one of the girls.

"Sure. We're hunters and seafarers as well as farmers. The furs you were sitting on in the wetu? Those came from somebody's dinner. So did most of our clothes. We believe everything not made by man is alive and should be treated respectfully. That's how we survived here for fourteen thousand years," Summer spread out her hands. "By cooperating with the land and its creatures."

"But you killed the animals," said the other girl.

"We thanked them for their gifts, for giving us food and clothing. Nothing was wasted. Every life must end, and every death helps another life to grow."

"You killed the cowboys," said the little boy.

"That was not us." Summer's smile didn't falter. It struck Lydia that being a tour guide here must require superhuman patience. "Come on inside. I'll show you how our dugout canoes were used for fishing and even whaling. You remember when we looked at that one," she pointed behind the wetu, "I told you the creek is right out back? That's where the alewives come to spawn every spring, all the way from the ocean."

Lydia hung back to check out the ten-foot log the Wampanoags had hollowed into a canoe. *Every life must end, and every death helps another life to grow.* Did that apply to Harriet Benbow?

"Hey." It was Summer. "Sorry I didn't recognize you before. I see so many people . . ."

"Sure. Thanks for letting me tag along."

"Yeah, I gotta go in for the rest. Catch you later."

It sounded enough like an invitation that Lydia followed the others into the museum.

The grown-ups were spreading into the rooms to look at exhibits. The three children remained in the hall, peering into a glass case full of flint arrowheads and scrapers, steel knives, and stone tomahawks.

"Cool!" said the little boy. "Look, there's blood on it!"

In front of his nose lay a wood-handled, metal-headed hatchet like the one Chief Red Otter had carried at Tony's lunch. The wide end flared into a blade. The narrow end was shorter and tapered to a rounded point. Its coloring was uneven—could that be blood? More likely rust, Lydia thought, or stains from years of use, or shadows from the overhead light.

Still . . .

"Summer, do people use these things?" Stopping her in the doorway. "Do they belong to the museum, or can tribal members take them out?"

Summer's face didn't change, but her voice was cautious. "Everything in the museum belongs to the tribe."

"So, if somebody needed a grinding stone, they could walk in and borrow one?"

"They wouldn't. These are here to show visitors."

"Do you have a key to the case?"

"No. There's only one, upstairs in the office." She turned to the boy. "Most outsiders don't know that our ancestors made many kinds of tools, long before the Europeans came. If you lived here four hundred years ago, you'd have learned how to shoot a deer with those arrowheads, and skin it with that knife, and scrape the hide with those flat stones."

"Or shoot cowboys," the boy said hopefully.

"They didn't *shoot* them," his sister said with scorn. "They scalped them."

"The cowboys were way out West, not here," said Summer. "We didn't shoot or scalp anybody. Our people only killed animals, for food and clothing. We welcomed the settlers. We taught them how to survive."

As a guest on a private tour, Lydia wasn't about to dispute that. "So nowadays, if somebody needs a grinding stone—?"

"They'd use their own, or ask a neighbor. A lot of us have keepsakes passed down through the family."

Summer rejoined the group in the whaling room. Lydia lingered for another look at the arrowheads and scrapers. Yes, she thought, if you had the skills and a key to the case, you could do some serious damage with those.

The congressman's wife and in-laws were exclaiming over two large murals. In "Whale Harvest Ceremony," a warrior in the foreground addressed tribe members who faced him across a bonfire, a heap of pumpkins and other makings of a feast, and three dugout canoes. In the background, a whale carcass lay on a beach. "Whale Hunters in Ocean" showed three black-haired, copper-skinned men paddling a dugout canoe on a choppy sea, while a fourth man, standing in the prow, aimed a harpoon at the tail of a diving whale.

"It's got nothing to do with us," Summer replied to a question from the wiry man with the Nikon. "The casino is a business issue created by the federal government."

"That's why you wanted to be legally recognized as a tribe, though, right?" he countered. "So you could get a piece of that revenue stream, like the other Indians."

"Federal recognition is also a business issue created by the government. Of course we're grateful for Congressman O'Keefe's support. But we don't need a stamp from Washington to know who we are. We've been here fourteen thousand years. Only, if the new guys set up requirements for us to stay on our land, to build housing and schools and whatever, we have to respond to that."

"The government isn't forcing you to build a mega gambling, hotel, and entertainment complex."

"The government wants us to pay property taxes and income taxes. Sales taxes. Driver's-license fees. They want our kids to wear store-bought clothes and get high-school diplomas and jobs. This is a money-based economy." She held out one of the purple-and-white shells in her necklace. "They don't take wampum."

"Ha!" The photographer laughed appreciatively. "That's

for sure."

He moved away. Lydia stared at sepia photographs of noteworthy Wampanoag whalers and wondered what kind of schisms the casino question must be driving through the tribal family.

She followed Summer out to the hall to ask her. But Summer headed for the back door, where someone was pounding on the glass panes and hollering: *Open up! Let me in!*

Lydia couldn't hear much of their conversation through the six-inch crack in the door. What she could see was a man who appeared to be very old and unsteady on his feet, who'd come here to hang out with his friends. Summer spoke gently, trying to make him understand they weren't here. This house was the tribe's museum. It was closed. She was leading a private tour. His friends would be over at the new Community Center. Did he remember where that was?—on the other side of town?

"My own tribe!" he howled. "Won't let me in my own building!"

Lydia retreated to the whaling room. Apparently living in harmony with all the beings of the earth wasn't as simple as it sounded.

Chapter 15: Enigma

Edgar Rowdey, emerging from his car, marveled at how many white elephants had found new homes over the weekend.

Yesterday morning he'd gazed across this patch of lawn at lamps and vases, skillets and salad spinners, baby clothes and video games, tennis racquets and fishing tackle. Now only a few half-empty tables remained, huddled together near the driveway.

A lady in a beach chair and a sun hat lowered her cell phone to wave. "Last chance for bargains!"

She was younger and cheerier than the woman who'd sold him the toastrack. Edgar sauntered toward her. "You've had a good sale."

"Yup. Just about cleaned out. Anything you like, make me an offer."

"Cleaned out by shoppers, I hope. Not burglars."

She laughed.

"What do you do with it all overnight? At the start, when you had so much."

"Oh, gosh. Betty moved her stuff into the garage. I was going to, but my son said, Mom, why? You want it gone, right? And I had to admit . . ."

She laughed again. Edgar chuckled and asked, "You left the tables out? Did items disappear? Or reappear?"

"Not that I noticed." She picked up a tattered magazine to fan herself. "You looking for anything particular?"

"There was a silver toastrack that caught my eye," said Edgar.

Her forehead wrinkled. He described it. "Doesn't ring a bell," she said. "Sorry."

"Oh well." He pushed up his glasses. "You snooze, you lose."

➤➤

A few miles away at The Whistling Pig, Brad Gerber asked Detective Pete Altman the same question. "You looking for anything particular?"

Altman had interrupted his Sunday to deliver the bad news in person. Sitting at a deck table, out of earshot of other customers, he confirmed: the police were now treating Harriet Benbow's death as a homicide.

Normally he'd have called on the victim's employer-slash-fiancé at home. It was Gerber who chose this gingerbread bar-restaurant up the street from Leo's Back End. His home, he told Altman, was full of bereaved family and friends who'd gathered for a goodbye brunch. Whatever the medical examiner had found, Harriet wouldn't have wanted it to wreck Lanie's memorial celebration.

They faced each other over coffee. The cause of death was hemorrhage, Detective Altman reported. Ms. Benbow must have been standing in the front hall when an assailant struck several blows to her face and neck, rupturing numerous blood vessels and knocking her backward against the kitchen island. The blows had also loosened her hairpiece, which the attacker grabbed and ripped off. Her head hit the rough granite edge of the counter top. She collapsed on the floor bleeding heavily, and died without regaining consciousness.

"Hard to say," Altman answered Gerber's question. "The M.E. describes the weapon as a metal object with a blunt point, thicker and shorter than a knife. Best guess, something like a poker, only not as heavy. Wielded with a stabbing motion, not swung like a baseball bat."

He didn't repeat Detective Adrienne Hall's analogy: "Like if you were a piñata and I didn't have a stick, so I grabbed a pointy rock and punched the candy out of you."

Brad Gerber remained hunched over his mug, staring down into his coffee. "Who did this? Any idea?"

"We're investigating a number of leads. It looks more like a crime of opportunity than premeditated murder. The security system—"

"So, a burglary gone wrong."

"That's one possibility. I have to ask you, same as everyone else. Where were you Friday evening, seven to ten PM?"

"I was at home. Mourning my late wife with some of our guests."

"And your daughter?"

"Rosalie, yes, of course." He looked up. "Harriet didn't join us. She'd have been welcome, but she was concerned about being a distraction."

"A distraction?"

"Her relationship with us had changed over time. Most of these folks only knew her as a GreenHome employee."

"Not as your fiancée."

Gerber's eyes narrowed. "We agreed to keep that to ourselves. I hope I can count on the police to respect our privacy."

"We'll do our best, Mr. Gerber."

"Someone told my daughter that Harriet was scalped."

"I'm sorry. If any of my guys said that, they shouldn't have. But you know," Altman gestured at hedges, houses, and passing cars, "this is a small town with an overactive grapevine. You get a suspicious death at a place like SailPort Landing, there's no way to keep it quiet. Let alone a victim whose hairpiece has gone missing."

"A hairpiece. I don't understand that." He grimaced. "Rosalie said, like a toupée? What makes you think Harriet had one? I never . . .?"

In his mind Detective Altman saw the barely recognizable face of the woman this man had expected to marry: the thickly crusted dried blood on her dark curls, the headband caught around one ear, the bruises and gashes from her scalp to her collarbone. He said carefully, "We found a carrying case, a stand, and other evidence. I'm told it's not unusual for ladies to wear what they call a topper to make their hair look thicker."

"But it's gone."

"Yes. Thanks for helping Detective Hall with our list of her missing belongings."

"So where are you on this? Any of it? What's your theory?"

"No theory yet. First we need more facts. We have search teams combing the area, officers checking evidence, conducting interviews, experts analyzing data, comparing similar cases, you name it. This is just the beginning, Mr. Gerber. Each new piece of information has a ripple effect. Right now we're asking if this looks like a home invasion that went off the rails, but it's too soon to rule much of anything in or out."

Before Gerber could digest that and interrupt again, Altman asked him, "Where is your daughter? I'll need to speak with her as well."

"Rosalie's looking after our guests. Best time to talk to

her is tomorrow. Or this afternoon after they leave, before she goes sailing. She keeps a little Dyer Dhow at the house. Can't go out very far, the bay's too rough, but she claims it's a better tranquilizer than Valium. Harriet said Rosalie's the most physical client she ever treated, as far as coping with stress. Same as her mother. They'd always rather sail or ride a bike or play tennis than talk."

A waitress came out with a fresh pot of coffee. "What is Rosalie's role in SailPort Landing?" Altman asked, leaning back for a refill.

"She's GreenHome's chief operating officer." Gerber covered his mug. "Titles don't mean that much. Like, Lanie and I had a goal of water access for residents, how to configure the road and the fence and so forth. Harriet confirmed we couldn't get Plan A past the town, and Rosalie figured out a Plan B we could live with."

"Your guests. I'll need names and addresses. And a couple minutes with anyone who arrived before Friday evening."

"No problem."

As soon as the waitress went inside, Altman asked, "Mr. Gerber, you said Harriet Benbow treated your daughter as a client?"

"Right. She was Rosalie's therapist up in Cambridge, when her marriage started going south five or six years ago. Harriet helped her so much that when Lanie's cancer came back, Rosalie called her. Did she mean what she'd said about wanting to change careers? And did her interest in real estate fit with Lanie needing an assistant?" Brad Gerber lifted his mug. "Perfect match."

"You liked her from the start?"

"I couldn't believe what a difference she made to Lanie.

So, to GreenHome."

"When did you and she decide to marry?"

"Me and Lanie? Oh, Harriet and me. Two days ago." Gerber paused to drink coffee and recall. "After that lunch with Harrington. He'd squired her and Rosalie all over town in that convertible of his, Tony's grand tour he called it. She came into Leo's all smiles, and Tony kept flirting with her, and I didn't care for that. Unprofessional. I dropped by the townhouse to tell her. She said, basically, So make me an offer I can't refuse. And I did."

"You gave her your wife's ring."

"Not then. I had it back at the house. We agreed she wouldn't wear it until we told Rosalie." Brad Gerber's already stony face stiffened. "But we didn't get the chance."

"So your daughter still doesn't know you planned to marry her best friend?"

"No. What would be the point? We've got way too much on our plates. I couldn't see adding one more thing." He frowned as if appealing for Altman to understand. "Scattering my wife's ashes. All our old friends here. We're running on empty, Rosalie and me both. And on top of that, GreenHome barreling along like a semi. Wheels turning. Decisions to make. I don't have time for any of this." He downed the rest of his coffee. "Thanks for the information, detective. Keep me posted."

Chapter 16: Toastrack

Driving home from Mashpee, Lydia realized she and Edgar hadn't retrieved the toastrack from Leo's mantelpiece last night.

OK. Lemons, lemonade. If she picked it up now, she could ask him what he thought about the tomahawk in the Wampanoag Museum. Edgar shrank from giving straight answers, but he had a way of sizing things up from his own angle that was just as useful. Things, for instance, like an antique tool which might or might not be bloodstained, and might or might not be the same one Chief Red Otter carried at Tony's luncheon.

Not that she believed any cousin of Mudge's would murder Harriet Benbow. Much less scalp her. For threatening to steal a big chunk of his tribe's land and build luxury housing for strangers? How old a cliché was that?

Lydia turned her Morris Minor off Main Street, AKA Route 6A, AKA Old King's Highway, into the driveway that ran past Louise French's office and Sparkle Jewelers. Crossing the long parking lot toward the Back End, she passed only one vehicle: a battered pickup truck.

Leo's front door was closed but not locked. "Hey, Mudge."

He stood at the sink, hand-washing dishes. "Hey, Lydia."

"Didn't you get the memo? It's Sunday."

"Yeah." He looked tired but cheerful. "How come you're not at the beach?"

Behind him she spotted the bowl and beaters from Leo's industrial-strength mixer, muffin tins, assorted spatulas, knives, and wooden spoons. "I went to check out that museum you recommended in Mashpee."

"They're closed. You should've asked me."

"I got lucky." She sidled past the register into the kitchen. "Your sister Summer was giving a private tour for Congressman O'Keefe and his family. She's good. I learned a lot."

"Did she tell you about O'Keefe and his buddies in D.C. cutting a deal where we could have our tribal sovereignty if we swore not to build a casino on the Cape Cod side of the bridge?"

"No." Lydia grabbed a dishtowel. "This was more about history."

"You don't think that's history?"

"History like, whaling. Dugout canoes. Growing crops. Tool-making. Do you remember the tomahawk Chief Red Otter was wearing on his belt at Tony's lunch?"

Another muffin tin clattered onto the pile in the dishrack. "Did Summer tell you he carved that handle himself?"

"I didn't ask. I wanted to know about the tomahawk in the glass case that looked exactly like it. The congressman's kid thought there was blood on it."

"If there was, it's from a three-hundred-year-old rabbit." Mudge rinsed soap off his hands. "So you didn't hear the story of how Red Otter got his name."

"No."

"Some of our people have been reviving our language. Wôpanâak. It got killed off the same time as that rabbit. Long story, but anyways, when Red Otter was a kid, he went by his Anglo name. Harold Potter."

"Uh-oh," said Lydia.

"Yeah. At first, the books coming out, it was kinda cool. But then, the movies. When my dad resigned and wanted him to take over, he couldn't be Chief Harry Potter. So, there's a line in this old Wôpanâak translation book: 'The otter is red.' First Harry's like, what? And then he goes, That's it! My name will be Chief Red Otter."

Lydia snapped her dishtowel at Mudge. "You made that up."

"No." He dodged, laughing. "It's true! I swear by the Sorcerer's Stone."

"OK, then. What's the truth about this?" She waved her towel at the stacked muffin tins on the counter. "What the Hollandaise are you cooking up, Mudge, all by yourself in Leo's kitchen on a Sunday?"

"Not *all* by myself. I cut a deal with Rosalie Gerber. I'll bake two dozen cranberry-corn muffins for your mom's memorial brunch, and GreenHome will give the tribe back our land."

"Holy molé! Are you—? A hundred-and-thirty-acre golf course for twenty-four muffins?"

"It's not a golf course, Lydia. It's a sacred Wampanoag burial ground. GreenHome promised years and years ago they'd deed it over to us. The muffins were just . . ."

"Payback for Manhattan?"

He laughed. "A thank-you present. From me to Rosalie in honor of her mother. Who I didn't know, but she was a good friend."

Lydia started shelving bowls. At the risk of dampening the mood, she had to ask: "Unlike Harriet Benbow?"

"I didn't know her either," Mudge returned. "And I didn't scalp her, if that's what you're asking."

"If I was, would I have walked in here with you and a couple hundred knives? How did you hear she was scalped?"

"Rosalie told me last night. I thought she was just being . . . I mean, what kind of psycho would do that? I can sort of see wanting to kill somebody . . ."

Lydia hadn't heard much after his first sentence. The responses that rose to her lips she stuffed back down again. *Did you spend the night with Rosalie? A real-estate developer? nearly twice your age? who's probably on the cops' list of top ten murder suspects?*

Eventually she said, "I heard it from Edgar. Leo called him from the police station after he sprung Tony. No source, no details. Did you get any from Rosalie?"

Mudge shook his head. "She heard it from Tony."

"Any idea what it means?"

He lifted a mixing bowl and twirled it on his fingertips— a trick that disarmed her every time. "Somebody's trying to frame the Indians?"

➤➤

The Right Honourable Tiberia Wormbold owed her late arrival at Sir James and Lady Dropthmore's lawn party to a feckless pod of right whales which had taken a wrong turn as the Queen Mary entered the Strait of Xiphopagus.

Yes. That would do. A lawn party.

After weeks of toying with possible settings for "The Toastrack Enigma," Edgar Rowdey had lost patience. If he didn't sweep distractions aside and buckle down to work, the dratted story would never get itself written. Certainly not in time for *Golden Age Mysteries'* tribute to Agatha Christie.

He'd survived enough stories not to fret unduly over this one. Once he settled on *where* and *who*, the thing would take on a life of its own. Plot elements would sprout. His current phase—*What mad fit induced me to agree to this foolishness?*—might recur, but not as intensely as now.

The question remained: Could he sweep distractions aside?

His custom was to list them and proceed to cross them off. *Ask vet about cat food. Transfer money for insurance bill. Have someone (Lydia?) fix wobbly table leg.* That didn't seem likely to work this time. Not when his list was topped by *Extract Tony from Exmouth Police crosshairs.*

What a pity he and Lydia hadn't stopped at Leo's last night to pick up the toastrack. If he could look at it while he worked . . .

That was an item he could cross off in ten minutes.

Still, it wouldn't get the baby bathed. He knew himself well enough to recognize that a MacGuffin sitting on his desk would be no match for a Sword of Damocles hanging over his head. How could he come to grips with "The Toastrack Enigma" if he couldn't look forward to setting it aside for his twice-daily breaks at the Back End? He didn't ask for much. A simple meal, a bit of gossip, a few laughs . . . a sanctuary he could no longer count on, thanks to the fracas Tony had churned up. Not until someone solved Harriet Benbow's murder.

By rights that should be Detective Altman and his colleague Detective Hall. Alas for procedure! The police, poor bunnies, were hobbled by the same rules and paperwork that empowered them. Investigative miracles such as fingerprint elimination and DNA matching might take days, if not weeks. Only when the proper boxes were checked could they confirm that although Tony Harrington had acted foolishly, to say the least, he'd stopped short of homicide.

By then Leo would have escalated from outrage to panic, and "The Toastrack Enigma" would look like the dog's dinner.

What the murderer might have got up to, Edgar dared not imagine.

No, there was no help for it. With a shudder of reluctance he lifted the receiver of his black telephone and dialed a number.

➤➤

The Back End's front door slammed open so hard that Lydia dropped a wooden spoon.

Tony Harrington stomped down the hall toward the kitchen, shouting: "Who's in here?"

"Hey, man." Mudge stepped out to meet him. "What's up?"

"Are you OK?" Lydia called from the sink.

Tony planted both hands on the counter. "What are you doing here?"

Not one of his best days, Lydia judged from his tousled hair, rumpled shirt, and irritated scowl. Still, nowhere near as bad as yesterday.

"Coffee?" she offered.

He lowered himself onto a stool. She slid over a mug. "So, what's happening?"

"I asked you first."

Mudge explained: Rosalie Gerber, departing guests, memorial brunch, muffins. "I called Leo, but he wasn't—"

Tony cut him off. "Has Edgar Rowdey been here?"

"Not today."

Oh, crêpes, the toastrack! thought Lydia. How did I

forget? She edged discreetly across the kitchen until she could see the mantelpiece. Safe! Its tarnished silver arches filled the space between a plaster skull and Dinah's favorite sign: *Unaccompanied Children Will Be Sold.*

Tony didn't seem to notice. She'd grown so used to fending off his flirtations that it felt a little creepy to see him hunched over his coffee, lost in his own thoughts.

Guilty thoughts? Could that man—her boss's son, her co-worker these past two months—have killed Harriet Benbow?

Mudge stepped toward the counter as if he intended to ask him. "You told Rosalie the cops said Harriet Benbow was scalped."

Tony looked up.

"What does that mean? What did they do to her?"

"Don't ask me. Ask your detective pal Pete Altman." He folded his arms behind his cup. "Or, hey, why don't you ask Rosalie? That was a slick move, bribing her with muffins to hand over her golf course." He chuckled. "Good luck."

"It's not her golf course. It's a Wampanoag burial ground."

"Whatever."

Lydia had watched this male faceoff, the old bull teasing the young stag, over and over since July. What bothered her this time wasn't their combative tone but the real combat underneath it. Backed into too tight a corner, would Tony switch from words to fists? Yes. Or a knife, or a meat hammer, or any weapon he could reach. And this time Mudge might run out of patience.

"What's your point?" she stepped in. "Don't trust Rosalie to keep her end of the bargain?"

"My point is it doesn't matter."

"To you, maybe." Mudge wasn't backing down.

Tony leaned toward him. "It doesn't matter who owns it. A hundred-and-thirty-acre parcel of prime waterfront? The Wampanoags or GreenHome, somebody's going to build something. Not a casino, that's off the table, but housing? Retail and commercial space?"

"So now you're the expert on Indian land."

"I'm an expert on real-estate development. That's why I hosted that luncheon. And if you didn't notice, Harriet Benbow saw the same thing as I did. Lanie Gerber drove GreenHome off a cliff. Dying of cancer for how many years? Brad and Rosalie couldn't cope. They sat around doing diddly-squat while Lanie hung onto those last two big parcels like a life raft. All ideas and no action. Harriet got there too late. They'd already missed their window to build SailPort Landing. Mashpee was her last stand."

"What, like General Custer?" Mudge folded his arms. "Is that an accusation?"

"Hey, if you can't stand the heat, get out of the kitchen."

Mudge whipped off his apron. Lydia grabbed his arm. Tony hadn't finished.

"You ever walk that golf course? Or look at the planning and zoning maps? I have. The burial ground's only one small part of it. And you know what? Bones can be moved."

"Says you. The wheel-greaser."

"Not just me. You and Chief Red Otter might be dreaming of a home where the buffalo roam, but Carl Hammond's hearing the sweet *ka-ching* of paying off the lawyers who got you guys federal recognition and are still trying to get you a casino. Hey, and how about some payback for the neighbors who dragged you through the courts? Guess what, ladies and gents! This tribe is a sovereign nation. With ancient fishing rights. Whaddya say we put a fish-processing plant on the ninth hole? Canning factory in the old clubhouse? Fertilizer in the pro shop?"

It was too comical to be horrifying, but too horrifying to be funny. Lydia sneaked a glance at Mudge. His blank face didn't tell her if he was stifling a laugh or an urge to slice those dark curls off the top of Tony's head.

"Why should you care?" he said. "You can't expedite anything in Mashpee."

Tony leaned back. A grin twitched the corner of his mouth. "I hear there may be a job opening at GreenHome LLC."

Chapter 17: Unraveling

Only Tony, thought Lydia, would try to parlay being a murder suspect into a step up the career ladder. Mudge guffawed. Tony erupted from his stool, and Mudge scooted out the door. Bye! He'd promised Rosalie he'd come back for the muffin baskets and maybe go sailing.

Tony's fist pounded the counter, rattling the condiments. Lydia was debating whether to hide in the ladies' room or grab the toastrack and run when the front door banged again. "Yoohoo!"

"In here," Tony snarled.

Edgar Rowdey ambled inside, a lanky white-bearded sunbeam in his familiar blue shirt and khaki shorts. "Mudge is in an awful hurry," he observed. "Were you two tormenting him?"

"I wasn't," Lydia said.

"Lock the door behind you," Tony growled.

"It's warming up," said Edgar. "Indian summer all over again."

Lydia, who'd started collecting his creative ways of saying no without actually saying no, added one more to her list.

"Sorry to keep you waiting," Edgar told Tony. "I ran into Louise French. Couldn't tear myself away."

With a glance at Lydia, Tony asked, "You want to go in the back?"

"Oh, why don't we stay here." Edgar plopped onto a counter stool. "I don't suppose there's iced coffee?"

"Coming right up." Lydia went to the fridge, smiling to herself.

"Such an awful shock," she heard Edgar say. "Walking in the door and finding her employer dead on the floor. I hadn't realized it was Harriet Benbow who asked Mrs. French to gussy up those three townhouses to open or show or whatever it is they do."

"It wasn't," Tony stated. "Harriet was just the messenger. Brad Gerber kept trying to kick the can down the road, and Louise French proposed the realtors' tour. She agreed with Harriet: time to fish or cut bait. First priority, get SailPort Landing out from under the red tape. The idea wasn't to sell the model condos, just stage them to start the ball rolling. Bring in some top agents; pump up the grapevine. Building to a reality check over a luncheon hosted by Harrington Associates. Because, face it: GreenHome had zero chance of making Lanie's dream a reality without my help."

"Mm," said Edgar. "Any-hoo. My heart went out to Mrs. French, poor bunny. She'd just checked that condo from top to bottom a few days ago and it was spotless. She had no idea Miss Benbow had moved in for the weekend."

"Alone?" Lydia couldn't resist asking.

"Don't look at me," Tony retorted.

"For that I expect we can count on the police." Edgar sipped his iced coffee. "Poking into what time she arrived, who she saw, how she spent Friday afternoon. With your help, Tony, to fill in the gaps."

"Not me. I didn't see her again after lunch."

Then why did you say— Lydia almost objected. No. This was Edgar's inquiry.

"Well, and before lunch," he said, "your tour of Quansett for her and Miss Gerber. Did you mention that in your police interview? Your friendly dispute at the yard sale?"

Tony hesitated. Lydia knew him well enough to see that he smelled a trap and was calculating how to dodge it.

Edgar, who'd known him for decades, added, "Over a silver toastrack?"

"I don't . . . Are you talking about that thing you brought in here yesterday?"

"It's an enigma!" Edgar declared. "How Miss Benbow could whisk it away on Friday, only for it to whisk itself back there the next morning. I wondered if you had any thoughts."

"Sorry," said Tony with a thin smile.

"Or if you might have offered that little dust-up as your reason for stopping by SailPort Landing on Friday evening. To ask Miss Benbow for an explanation. Why she pounced on a yard-sale toastrack that both her friends wanted. But you had other reasons for calling on her?"

"No. I didn't. Call on her." Hearing how brusque he sounded, Tony tried for an airier tone. "Harriet was busy Friday evening. After my luncheon she wanted to look up some town records in Mashpee. Then she and Brad and Rosalie were going to the yacht club for dinner. I went home to write up my notes and think about next steps."

"You stopped at a package store for a fifth of Glen Something-or-other."

"And chugged most of it." Another forced smile. "You saw what shape I was in yesterday morning."

Edgar sloshed his ice cubes around in his glass. "Tony, I've never seen you drink anything more exotic than Dewar's. What is this in aid of? What sinister conclusions do you imagine the police would draw if you admitted you'd dropped by with a gift for a lady you hoped to work with?"

"I didn't see Harriet again after lunch! How many times do I have to say it?"

"Oh, for pity's sake. You've no need to deceive me, and no hope of deceiving the police. Even as we speak they're matching the blood on that floor to the blood on your shoes. Identifying all the follicles and fingerprints and so forth you'll have strewn around the condo."

Tony said heatedly, "I told them, Harriet invited me in on Friday morning to help find her cell phone. So, yeah. I left prints and whatnot all over the condo. So what? The point is, whoever killed her, it wasn't me."

"The point is," Edgar countered, "if you lie to the police about a harmless bottle of Scotch, why should they believe you about anything?"

"OK. You tell me, then. What horrible crimes did I commit that I'm lying about?"

Edgar set down his glass with a sigh. "Tony. Your lunch was a triumph. You'll concede that? You can't have expected to come away with a signed contract on the spot. Not with Brad and Rosalie Gerber distracted by their memorial. Miss Benbow, being part of the company but not the family, seized her moment. Yes? She installed herself at SailPort Landing on Thursday afternoon, and with a hand from you, set about knitting up the loose ends."

Tony was staring at Edgar as if he'd pulled a Queen of Diamonds out of his ear. "Where'd you get this? You never met Harriet Benbow. Did you?"

"Heavens no. I don't know any of these people. I'm utterly unbiased. Aside from a desire to see this mare's nest untangled without ensnaring any more victims."

"What do you mean, any more victims?"

"Hm. Well, you know, this investigation started as something of a dragnet, scooping up whatever suspects and evidence happened to fall in. You, for instance. So far you've had some luck explaining away the more circumstantial items, like your fingerprints in that condo. But once they catch you in a lie—"

"I'm innocent until proved guilty, Edgar. That's the law. The cops can't prove I'm guilty when I'm not."

"The net will tighten. It's less a matter of proof than assumptions. Should they cross you off their list or keep a close eye on you?" Before Tony could retort, Edgar added, "As long as you're hogging the spotlight, you're helping someone who doesn't deserve it. Who's already murdered one person and might not stop there."

"Whoa," Tony growled. "Hold on."

Lydia was too impatient to hold on. "Edgar! Do you know who killed Harriet?"

"I wouldn't say *know*. There are only so many possibilities."

"For God's sake!" Tony slapped both hands on the counter. "Cut to the chase! Who?"

Edgar looked at him over the rims of his glasses. "Why don't you tell me what happened when you went to SailPort Landing on Friday with your bottle of Scotch."

➻

It took Tony three tries. To explain Friday night, he had to back up to Friday morning. Or, no. Back up to Thursday.

Harriet painted herself as the practical one at GreenHome. The invisible hand that kept the wheels turning. Hah! Invisible? Harriet Benbow cared as much about presentation as any female. Clothes, hair, makeup, jewelry—

Anyhow, point being, she had a thing about sending mixed signals. Throwing people off balance.

So, Tony called her Thursday night to confirm their date Friday morning, and Harriet said Why don't you come over now? She'd figured out a coat-tailing hack for the security camera at the gate and she needed a guinea pig. Wait for Mario's pizza-delivery guy and sneak in behind him. Oh, and bring beer.

Over a Sam Adams and a spinach-and-mushroom with extra garlic, he asked Why the hack? Don't you control the in-and-out list on your phone? Harriet said she was camping at SailPort Landing for two reasons: privacy and elbow room. Brad and Rosalie Gerber had promoted her to business manager because they needed her to manage their business. She couldn't do that with kibitzers breathing down her neck. Was it anybody else's affair if she got to Quansett a few hours early, and chose pizza on the deck with Tony over lobster with a bunch of long faces at the Yacht Club?

Harriet adored Lanie Gerber—truly, one of the dearest souls who ever walked the planet. Everybody adored Lanie. But, face it. Her dying wishes took GreenHome LLC down with her. It was like she rejected the twenty-first century. Forget environmental regulations: Quansett's last stretch of untouched waterfront was meant to be SailPort Landing! Forget the glitch in the Indian Recognition Act of 1934 that hamstrung the Mashpee Wampanoag tribe: Lanie recognized who owned that golf course, whether the law did or not!

That was then, said Harriet. This is now. Time to pull up our socks and move on.

"I'd never seen this side of her before," said Tony. "Open, excited, but relaxed, you know? Drinking beer and eating pizza under the stars, talking like we'd known each other forever." He shook his head. "I thought it was me."

You would! thought Lydia, standing out of sight next to the fridge.

Tony's hopes got their first kick in the shin when he sidled closer to Harriet and moved in for a kiss. She pushed him away, laughing. *Not tonight, garlic-breath!* Tomorrow then? *Maybe. We'll see how it goes.*

In the morning he drove over early. She made him wait outside in his car. Rosalie had already arrived for their historical tour of Quansett. They'd invited Brad, too, but he had a golf date.

WTF? Tony bristled, and fumed, and started flirting with Rosalie.

The you-know-what hit the fan at the yard sale.

What did he care about somebody's castoff silverware? Arguing over the toastrack was an excuse to tease Rosalie. Get to know her better. If that put Harriet's nose out of joint, tough luck. But, damn! Why'd she want to turn a friendly skirmish into a power struggle?

So, fine. Point made, point taken. Don't mess around with Harriet Benbow. No worries. They could still do business, and pleasure too.

But when the three of them met Brad and the two Wampanoags for their luncheon at the Back End, Harriet's control issues got totally out of hand.

Up till that moment she had said not one word, dropped not one hint, about moving the condo project from Quansett to Mashpee. She waited until the pause between sandwiches and dessert to slip it into the conversation. So vaguely that he thought he'd misunderstood. Until he saw Rosalie's face frozen in shock. The Indians must've been poleaxed, although they hid it. Brad Gerber? Tony couldn't tell. He doubted Harriet would throw such a curve without her boss's approval. Not approval of making the switch, necessarily, but seeing what reaction it would get.

"What reaction did it get?" Edgar asked.

"What you'd expect. Everybody hated it."

Lydia was about to step out and object—*That's not what you told Mudge and me!*—when Edgar inquired, "How could you tell?"

Tony sounded startled. "How could I tell? This was a one-eighty from the plans we'd come there about. For me, working with GreenHome to steer SailPort Landing through the approval process. For the Wampanoags, getting back their land." He paused. "If you're asking me, Did anybody jump on the table yelling *I'll kill you, Harriet Benbow*? No. Of course not. We were all up the same creek. Nobody was gonna show their cards until we knew what game she was playing."

"You saw it as a game because she'd played snatch-the-bacon with the toastrack," Edgar observed (charitably, in Lydia's opinion). "Did you tell the police about that?"

"I told the police nothing. They didn't ask. *We know you murdered Harriet Benbow. That's her blood in your car, right? You went over there to get laid and she said no. So you attacked her. Bashed her face and smashed her head against the counter. Right?* Yeah. Like I'd fall for that crap. Guys I went to school with! You know what I told them? One thing. Talk to my lawyer."

"They didn't ask you about the Scotch?"

"Hell no. They had it all figured out. Pin the tail on the donkey. Me or Chief Red Otter or Frosty the Snowman. Whoever they could make the shoe fit."

"Hm," said Edgar thoughtfully. "But you did buy that bottle for her. As a foot in the door, so to speak. What with her hints the night before that you'd be welcome."

"Well, yeah." Lydia couldn't see his face, but she heard Tony's relief that somebody understood. "I knew she had a thing for single-malt Scotch. Harrington Associates' motto: be creative and be persistent."

"What time did you go over there?"

"A little past five. To catch her between leaving Mashpee Town Hall and meeting Brad and Rosalie for dinner. They'd been up since dawn scattering ashes in Lanie's rose garden, so they planned an early night. But she wasn't there. So I hung it on her doorknob with a note tied with a ribbon."

"Saying you'd call her?"

"Saying, call me or I'll come by later." A harsh note crept into Tony's voice. "I waited till nine-thirty. I called, I texted, no answer. I came back, saw her car was in the driveway and the gift bag was gone. So I rang the bell. Nada. I tried the door and it opened."

He halted. Lydia moved out so she could watch him as well as listen. His face looked almost as grim as yesterday morning.

"She was lying in a mess of blood. I saw when I stepped into the hall. I mean, I'm no expert, but she was dead. No question. Her head torn up, and her face . . ." Tony shuddered. "Like she was attacked by a pack of wolves. Kind of pushed up against the kitchen island. The granite top had blood on it, too. And my bottle of Scotch, sitting there with my note tied to the neck."

Again he stopped. Edgar waited placidly.

"I had to get it back."

"Mm." Edgar nodded.

"I couldn't help her. It was too late. I just stood there trying to wrap my brain around this, this nightmare. Like quicksand sucking me in and I couldn't stop it. Like I was falling into a slow-motion train wreck, my future, the cops, news media, all my plans and hard work flushing down the toilet. All I could think was, Go! Grab that bottle with my fingerprints on it, and find the gift bag, and get the hell out of here." He caught sight of Lydia and finished, "So I did. That's the truth. So help me God."

Lydia, groping for a response, came up with the one she gave disgruntled Back End customers. "I'm so sorry."

Edgar said, "I should think this will save Detective Altman hours, if not days, of chasing red herrings down dead ends. One can only hope he'll be grateful."

Tony answered with a bitter chuckle. "Save me going broke to pay Fred Jones."

"I take it you haven't spoken any further with your other luncheon guests. About Miss Benbow's death, or about your business dealings?"

"You mean while I was in police custody and they were cruising around on their yacht? No."

"Or the Wampanoags?" Edgar continued unperturbed. "In person or through Mudge? Any news or rumors from Miss Benbow's search for documents or whatever in Mashpee?"

"Ask Mudge."

"Hm. Sunday afternoon. He'll be working at the Frigate?"

"Not today." Lydia was itching to get Edgar alone and find out how much of Tony's story he believed. "He came here to bake muffins for the Gerbers' memorial brunch. That's where he was going when you saw him. To pick up the serving baskets."

Seeing Edgar's frown, Tony added, "No worries about finding him. The place'll be crawling with cops. Gotta grill those mourners before they escape over the bridge."

The furrows on Edgar's forehead and the angle of his bushy white eyebrows didn't soften as much as Lydia expected. "Will he come back here?"

"I doubt it," she said.

Tony said, "He's going sailing with Ro-o-osalie."

One of the eyebrows lifted. "Hummy hummy hoo."

"You can say that again. He's what, twenty? And she's like thirty-five?"

Lydia started to protest, but Edgar interrupted. "Pass me the phone, would you?"

She slid it across the counter. Pushing buttons, he said, "Tony, will you close up here?"

"Why?"

"I must be off. Pressing matters to attend to and so on."

Chapter 18: Sailing

No tool in a detective's kit is more valuable, Pete Altman thought, than a wife who'll take the grandkids to Cap'n Chilly's for ice cream while you're trying to solve a murder.

Technically he wasn't trying to solve a murder so much as get his ducks in a row. Once the autopsy report came in, his suspicious death would become a homicide. Then the pace would pick up fast, as his team gathered to pool their findings and map out plans instead of sending texts and voicemails.

Right now his phone was so full that he was only returning messages that sounded urgent. Like State Police Detective Adrienne Hall's: *Call me ASAP.*

Hall's voice was breathless and staticky. She was driving, she said, navigating by GPS, so he'd have to do most of the talking. Nutshell preview: Tony Harrington and his attorney would meet them at the station tomorrow morning.

While Hall looked for a place to pull over, Altman gave her his own nutshell report. No news from the team interviewing the Gerbers' out-of-town guests before they headed home. Of course it was early yet, but they'd expected this would be more about ticking boxes than turning up red flags. For now, Tony still topped the Persons of Interest list.

Hall agreed. Personally, though, she had a hard time picturing Tony Harrington committing this crime. One of the officers dealing with his car told her she should've known him as a kid, shooting sparrows off telephone wires with a sling-shot. Yeah, OK, but bash up a fellow human being? Whole nother can of worms.

"I'm still wondering what kind of screwball killer lops off the victim's hairpiece," said Altman.

"As a matter of fact— Hold on, here's a turnout."

The call went dead. When Hall came back on, her voice was clear. "I asked Doc Rafferty about that. The scalping. He's not done with his report, but since we've got extenuating circumstances—"

"The scalping?" Altman interrupted.

"In a minute, Pete. First, yes. We're dealing with a homicide. And here's what's been holding it up. Point one, this was such a frenzied attack that it damaged a bunch of different blood vessels. Proximate cause of death is blood loss from arteries in the victim's neck and scalp. That's why so much blood on the floor. Point two: her hairpiece had nothing to do with it. Collateral damage. Point three: hitting her head on the counter ruptured a vein inside the skull, causing a subdural hematoma. Also lethal. This wasn't like shooting a bird with a slingshot. More like Hitchcock's *Birds*—a massive overdose of violence."

"Huh." Altman thought it over.

"The irony being, Ms. Benbow would have died no matter how you slice it, but not by, quote, scalping. Your PR gal at the station didn't call you about that? What's her name, Rita?"

"She might have." He remembered seeing Rita Bolt on his call list. "I haven't talked to her."

"That's the extenuating circumstances. The one thing we can pin on Tony Harrington for sure. He's been spreading it around that our victim was scalped."

"Oh, hell."

"Rita said she's working on a press release. All she could tell me was, Tony must have heard that at the station yesterday from somebody who saw the body."

"She doesn't know who?"

"Nah. Who's gonna cop to it? or point the finger? Half these guys have been buddies since kindergarten. Anyhow, too late now to put the genie back in the bottle. They've all got orders to cork it, pronto. Including Tony and Leo."

"I'll call Roger Cargill," Altman said. "The officer who's on both the Mashpee and the tribal police forces. See if he can set up a meeting with Carl Hammond and Chief Red Otter tomorrow. Try and walk this back."

"Right," Hall said. "The other thing is, what if there's something in it?"

"What do you mean?"

"Why did this perp tear off the victim's hairpiece? Was it meant to be a scalping? Or staged to look like one?"

"Gotcha. Could be some wacko sending a message. About what, though? Indians? Women with fake hair? SailPort Landing?"

"If we can't tell, it's not much of a message," Hall observed.

Altman sighed. "What else did Rafferty have to say?"

"Nothing. You know him. Like pulling teeth. After we hung up I called a friend who used to work at Plimoth Patuxet Museum. He said scalping wasn't a Wampanoag custom. I know, all those cowboy and Indian movies, but think about it. These were folks who killed animals for food and used every hair and claw. They didn't cut off the heads and hang them on the wall as trophies. Or their enemies' heads, either. That was the Europeans. The guillotine? Anne Boleyn? He said, the only time Indians scalped anybody was fighting for the French or the English. The deal was, they got paid by the head. Scalps were like an itemized bill."

"Well, I'll be darned," said Altman. His phone beeped; he ignored it. "The things they don't teach you in school."

"So, did our perp know this? And what did he figure we'd know? Are we looking for a smash-and-grabber who screwed up and then said to himself, OK, toupée, scalping, Indians, maybe the cops'll buy it? Or is this a premeditated murder that we're meant to blame on the Wampanoags? Or a sneaky double-fake by real Wampanoags who hoped we'd take it for a frame-up and cross them off the suspect list?"

Altman's phone was humming. "Good questions. Listen, I've got a call I need to take. Let's see what the afternoon brings us, and I'll get back to you tonight after my grandkids go home."

➦

The sail was a triangular rainbow. Rosalie's boat was so small it only had one. Following her down the walkway to the dock, Mudge couldn't believe she expected two full-grown adults to fit in that oversize wooden bathtub. He agreed with her this was a glorious day to get out on the water, but not if it meant interlocking knees.

Ten minutes later they were skimming over the blue-green rippled sea, grinning like a pair of clowns. She'd kept her unspoken promise and made no moves except to pilot the dinghy. There was leg room, barely; there were cushions to sit on; there were oars in case of emergency. There was no sound but the waves burbling under them and gulls crying overhead. Whether Rosalie was burned out after three days of memories, grief, condolences, et cetera, or if she just preferred sun and salt air and speed to conversation, the silence suited Mudge.

She'd ranted for a whole minute when he first arrived: how fed up she was with people obsessing about real-estate prices while they overlooked the land itself. Where did they get off calling it *real estate* if it was just numbers on a computer screen? What was the point of advertising wooded lots and then bulldozing the trees to install a lawn, expensively maintained till the end of time by underpaid immigrants armed with toxic chemicals? All that hype about cleaning up the environment with technology—didn't that drive him crazy, when what they really should do was admit they totally blew it back in the 1600s, and beg the few surviving natives for help?

Years of experience had taught Mudge the best answer was an appreciative chuckle. It wasn't for him to tell the lady who held the deed to his tribe's ancient burial ground what "they" should do. Or that if he had to grind flour with a mortar and pestle like his ancestors, forget about cranberry-corn muffins.

Anyhow, he was glad she cared. In spite of Tony's badgering, he believed Rosalie could be trusted to keep her word. Red Otter said they had her mother to thank, who'd taught her to dance between worlds, like the Wampanoags. Mudge understood that better now than he would have before he and Lydia started the Flying Wedge. His white caterer's apron was a backstage pass into the foreigners' world where Rosalie lived. Without it, if he'd parked his beat-up truck down the street and carried a shopping bag around her BMW, her dad's Lexus, and the cop cars in the driveway, somebody would have called 9-1-1 before he reached the front door.

The Gerbers hadn't stamped as heavy a mark on their piece of Quansett as their neighbors. Their cottage (or mansion, from Mudge's viewpoint) was a relic from the 1950s: white siding, green shutters, a flagstone walk lined with hydrangeas. Out back behind the rose garden, a rickety boardwalk ran through marsh grass to a small plank dock. No wonder they kept their schooner over at the Exmouth Yacht Club. This sheltered part of Fishhook Cove would be too shallow for anything much bigger than the three boats tied to the Gerbers' dock posts: Rosalie's wooden sailing dinghy, a fiberglass Boston Whaler with an outboard motor, and a green canoe which lay bottom-up beside a half-open trunk.

Before they clambered aboard, Rosalie tossed in two flotation cushions. Just as safe as life jackets, she declared, if you slipped your arms through the straps, and a lot more comfortable to sit on.

The air was so still on land that Mudge worried less about capsizing than getting stranded in the middle of the cove. The pair of oars on the floor made him think of slave-propelled galleys in late-night movies. Rosalie rubbed the mast for wind, and Mudge did, too. Moments later, a puff sent them scudding across the inlet.

Rosalie pumped a fist in triumph. Mudge raised his to bump hers.

"I needed this!" she hollered.

"Me too." He laughed. "Worth sweating over a hot oven."

"I'm so glad." He couldn't tell if she meant glad that he'd granted her wish or glad simply to be here, unshackled, flying with the wind. Probably both.

They were heading into the curve of Fishhook Cove: on their right a long shore of marsh, trees, docks, and houses, and on their left Fishhook Point jutting into Cape Cod Bay. That pale stretch between patches of woods must be the locals' private beach. Looking back, Mudge saw the little dock they'd come from. From out here on the water, the age-bleached posts of a dock and the bright cluster of boats around it marked where a house stood, usually higher up and half hidden by trees.

"Ready about," Rosalie announced. "Hard alee."

They both ducked so as not to be hit by the swinging boom that held the foot of the sail. Mudge wondered why Rosalie was zigzagging deeper into civilization instead of letting the wind carry them toward the shining open water.

"Why don't we go that way?" He pointed at the inlet's mouth.

"Rip tide. See the green can off the tip of the point? Pass that and we'd be swept straight out to sea."

He knew a can was a buoy, but he didn't see one. The point itself looked empty: no docks or houses, only an uneven skyline of trees topping a low cliff. "Is that a park or what?"

"That's SailPort Landing."

"Really?" Squinting, Mudge caught a flash of sun on glass, then glimpses of a silvery rooftop and a deck railing. "Prodigious!"

"My mom's favorite place," Rosalie nodded. "Besides her garden. Fishhook Point. She refused to build on it until we got a design that would keep it looking like that. Unspoiled."

Mudge was still trying to match the geography he was seeing from the water with the roadmap in his head. "I didn't know it was so close to your house."

"It isn't, unless you're a seagull. But I know what you're saying. By car the entrance gate's three miles away. You can't see from Main Street how Fishhook Point curves back into Quansett."

"You could sail there from your place in, what? Fifteen minutes?"

"I wish! That's what stalled the project—well, one thing. No water access. They wouldn't give us dock permits. Even though my mom owned the land since before I was born. Even though she was dying of cancer. She and my dad used to walk over there every Sunday, until last fall when it turned cold and her legs gave out." She shaded her eyes, checking the sail. "And all she got was grief. My last days on earth, she said, wasted by lobbyists and lawyers."

"I heard about the bike coalition. They sued, right? To keep the Ancient Way open to the public?"

"Ancient Way! Ancient deer track. Now it's a state-of-the-art asphalt walking-jogging-bike path. It doesn't even follow the old route, because once you add all the access requirements, it wouldn't fit. We had to move it across the creek and build a footbridge farther down. I mean, God forbid some jogger should lose track of his step count or heart rate for two seconds. And forget about building homes in harmony with the landscape. Adding value to the village." Rosalie yanked on the rope in her hand and the boat lurched. "Sorry. Don't get me started."

"No." With a smile of reassurance, Mudge turned away. He was happy not to talk. This hour of sanctuary was too short to waste on grievances. A six-hour shift of selling books at the Frigate felt like a bad joke.

"At least the new path let her keep on walking," said Rosalie. "Even though they couldn't go all the way out the Point anymore."

"The fence blocks off the old path?"

"Well yeah. That's the point. Ha ha! Pardon my pun."

"What about the last stretch, from the woods down to the marsh?"

Rosalie looked at him in surprise. "You've been there?"

"Sure." Mudge grinned. "Anyplace there's quahogs, I've been there. That's one of the best on the North Shore."

"I didn't know— I thought— Damn! My secret chowder spot! I wouldn't even take my rake and bucket, so nobody would guess."

"You don't need a rake and a bucket. You find them with your toes."

She mock-scowled. "Don't you have your own quahogs in Mashpee?"

He was laughing. "They're all our quahogs. Quahogs and Wampanoags, we go back together a thousand years. Shellfishing rights? That's the real Ancient Way."

"Yeah, well, and that's why there's a bush-and-boulder break at the end of the fence. For the deer, the raccoons and other furry mammals, and you. Anybody else"—she made a gun with her fingers—"*ka-pow!*"

Mudge stretched out his arms, half pretending to be shot, half embracing the landscape. Sun sparkled on the water. Distant docks and pilings lined the curved rim of the cove like a jaw full of crooked teeth. He didn't want to think about going back.

"Maybe I should give Tony a shot," said Rosalie. "What do you think? He's so juiced to fight the bureaucracy. Let him grease some wheels. Or palms. This is obviously all about politics, since doing the right thing got us exactly nowhere."

"You're not worried that Tony might've killed your friend?"

"Are you kidding? Tony, kill Harriet? No. No way." She shook her head so emphatically that her sunglasses tilted. "Is that what the cops are saying?"

"I don't think they're saying anything. Not yet. Not to me, that's for sure."

"Tony had the hots for Harriet. Partly business, but mostly . . ."

Mudge nodded. "Just being Tony."

"She told me he came knocking on her door the first night she got there, with a six-pack, hoping she'd ask him to stay over." Rosalie adjusted her sunglasses. "For all I know, maybe she did. There was definitely some voltage when he picked us up for the grand tour."

Mudge leaned back and trailed his hand in the water. "There was some voltage at that lunch, too."

"Who knows? But, y'know, who cares? You don't murder your negotiating partners in a business deal. If you don't like how it's going, you keep talking. No," Rosalie repeated. "I know the cops have their forms to fill out, protocol and all that, but it's crazy to think anybody who knew Harriet would kill her. This was some random psychopath. A burglar who thought he was hitting an empty condo. A homeless guy looking for a place to sleep. He sneaks in through the gate behind somebody's car, and whoa! Surprise!"

The wind had died down to a breeze. "Yeah," Mudge said. "I hate to say it, but we should start back."

Rosalie sighed. "I'd rather stay out here. Like, forever."

"Yeah." He smiled at her. "Me too. Except I'd lose my job."

"Well, OK then. Ready about."

He ducked.

"Hard alee."

Over swung the tiller in her hand. Over swung the boom and the rainbow sail. The boat slowed, turned, and headed toward SailPort Landing.

"It's totally different seeing it from the water," said Mudge.

"Yeah, well," Rosalie said. "No sails, no port, and no landing."

"It's not over, is it?"

"It is for my mom." Rosalie cleated off the main sheet. "So many things she loved that she had to give up." She coiled the rope's end with a studied fussiness Mudge recognized from the aftermath of his own mother's death. "Like the Tin Woodman—chopping off one piece of herself at a time."

"She liked having the new bike path, though."

"Sailing was the worst. A day like this . . . It killed her to stay inside. That's why she told us to scatter her ashes from Calliope, her schooner. I found an urn online she'd have loved. A little balsa-wood ship to carry her out to sea."

Rosalie's voice suddenly sounded too loud. The sail behind her flapped and fluttered. Mudge lurched over to grab the swinging boom before it hit her on the head.

"Uh-oh." She grimaced at him. "Our wind's died."

Chapter 19: Water Sports

Edgar Rowdey's distaste for telling other people what to do made him a favorite with the Back End staff. On the other hand, it meant they couldn't always guess what he wanted or how much he wanted it. On this particular Sunday afternoon, Lydia Vivaldi was pretty sure Edgar urgently desired Tony Harrington to leave so he could use Leo's phone in private.

She asked Tony if he'd like to go check on the frogs.

His look of surprise melted into a leer. "Is that like, come and look at my etchings?"

"No, it's like, let's go check on the frogs."

To be fair, the custom of keeping tabs on the population of Leo's miniature pond had stopped before Tony turned up here looking for a summer job. Lydia hoped Edgar appreciated what a sacrifice she was making. She was pleased to see two frogs perched on the rocks rimming the lily pads, but she'd much rather have stayed inside to eavesdrop.

"Yoo-hoo!"

They found Edgar clearing away their dishes, turning out the kitchen lights.

"So who were you so desperate to talk to?" Tony asked him.

"How are the frogs?"

"Healthy and hoppy." Tony chuckled. "Ribit!"

Lydia, who'd stayed by the door, held it open for Edgar.

"You two will lock up?" he asked.

"I'm coming with you." Lydia followed him down the walk.

"Wait for me!" Tony scrabbled with the latch.

"No," Lydia said.

"I've got errands to run," Edgar told them both. "People to see."

Lydia leaned on the hood of his VW wagon. "Your car or mine?"

"Don't leave me here!" Tony hollered. "The cops still have my Mustang!"

The loud click of unlocking doors was Lydia's cue to hop into Edgar's passenger seat. As they headed for the driveway, she waved to Tony out the window. "See you tomorrow!"

In the interest of not pushing her luck, she didn't ask Edgar where they were going. Turning right onto Main Street, he drove past the library and his house in silence.

"There will be police," he said when they stopped at Quansett's one traffic light. "You may have to get a taxi home."

"From where?" Lydia tried to recall if this was the way to Exmouth HQ. Edgar kept his eyes on the intersection and didn't answer.

When the light changed she asked, "You called Detective Altman?"

"Mm."

"Does he know who killed Harriet Benbow?"

"Heavens no. Not yet."

"But you do?"

"I wouldn't go as far as that. As I said before, there are only so many possibilities. Mr. Altman is more or less obliged to narrow them down methodically, by the book. The difficulty there . . ." He slowed for a cluster of children who threatened to drift into the road. "Is the risk of someone else being hurt."

"You mean, whoever attacked Harriet may strike again?"

"Well, exactly. I'm inclined to agree with him that Miss Benbow's assailant struck on impulse. A loose cannon, in detective parlance. Meaning that any offhand remark, however innocently intended, could light the fuse."

"So we're going where? Into the cannon's mouth?"

"Now, now. We're going to the Gerbers' house. No need for melodrama. Although . . ." For the first time he glanced at her. "I suppose we ought to have driven separate cars."

They turned left off Main Street onto a narrow road Lydia hadn't noticed before. "This would be a good time for you to fill in gaps," she said. "Like, who is the loose cannon? So I won't drop any inflammatory remarks."

"Dear, you do remember this is a police investigation." Edgar peered into the scrubby oaks and pines that almost brushed his windows. "You and I are mere civilians. Sometimes tolerated as spectators, but not welcome to join the fray, if any."

They emerged from the trees into a flat, sandy landscape dotted with houses which became larger and sparser as they neared the water. "Detective Altman doesn't know you're coming, does he."

"He's only just arriving himself," Edgar said. "His people have been interviewing the Gerbers' guests. Poor bunny, I could feel him shrink in horror when he heard my voice on the phone. But here we are," he twisted the wheel abruptly. "Heavens to Betsy. Just as well you didn't bring your car."

He was frowning at the driveway, jammed to overflowing by a Lexus, a BMW, and two police cruisers. On the street, sticking out like a sore thumb in a manicure parlor, sat Mudge's rusty old pickup truck.

"My civilian intuition tells me this is the Gerbers' house."

"Mm," said Edgar.

Lydia cringed as he pulled up bumper-to-bumper with an unmarked sedan which had to be Detective Altman's. When they got out, Edgar headed for the flagstone walk. Lydia started to ask if he didn't want to lock his car, but realized—maneuvering between police vehicles—he probably had weighed the odds and opted for a fast getaway.

"Mudge is here," she said instead. "If the cops give us a hard time, we can hang out with him."

"One can only hope." Edgar didn't sound optimistic.

➤➤

The water's rippled surface smoothed to glass. The limp rainbow sail wrapped itself around the mast like a towel around a wet swimmer.

Rosalie stood up and, with a hand shading her eyes, scanned the cove. Then she sighed, sat down again, and rubbed the mast below the boom.

Mudge figured that if this magic trick brought wind, it would help them more blowing into the sail than into the cockpit, and rubbed the mast above the boom.

"Grrr." Rosalie freed the rope she'd just cleated. The sail didn't move. She pumped the tiller back and forth. The dinghy inched forward.

School was still a recent enough memory for Mudge to welcome a good excuse for being late to work. Peace engulfed him. He adjusted the cushion between his back and the boat's hard wooden gunwale. His gaze rested on the vivid green of marsh grass and the darker green of trees onshore. SailPort Landing from the water reminded him of a picture that hung in the back room at the Back End. Painted by one of Leo's daughters . . . not Jackie. The younger one. Amber? Amy? This hot sun was making him too drowsy to recall her name. It couldn't be the same landscape, anyhow. Not unless she'd copied it from a photo. What artist would set up her easel in a boat? He studied the scene, looking for differences. Trying not to fall asleep. Those shaggy trees . . . You couldn't see the fence at all.

He registered Rosalie reaching down by their feet, wrestling with an oar, but his focus didn't shift until she hefted it in the air.

"You want a hand with that?"

She stared at him with wild angry eyes. "Too late."

The unexpected blow knocked him sideways and back. He kicked, struggling to regain his balance, to pitch forward and push her off, but she gripped his leg.

"Rosalie! What are you—?"

"I won't let you get away with this!"

She shoved him backwards in a somersault. He grabbed for the gunwale and missed, hitting it with his spine instead. Twisting in pain, he felt the dinghy tilt and his whole body with it. In seconds he was over the side, his arms and legs flailing, his head submerged, gasping for air, sinking.

Under water his head throbbed. His hand scraped against smooth wood. He groped higher and clung to the boat. The oar fell like a hammer on his fingers. He screamed. Chilly salt water filled his mouth. Coughing, choking, he fought back, thrashing for a hold on anything that would pull him up, grappling with the sea that was sucking him down.

He broke through into light. Gulps of air filled his lungs. The oar hit him again, shooting pain through his head and shattering his thoughts.

Mudge sank below the surface into cold dark silence.

→

A police officer blocked Edgar and Lydia from following Detective Altman to the Gerbers' dock. They'd sneaked around back after agreeing to finesse the front door. Lydia, peeking through the long windows, concluded the cop on guard there didn't plan to open up for anybody, least of all a pair of uninvited civilians.

Lanie's rose garden posed a thorny challenge. Hunting for a way through, they could hear male voices arguing. The two loudest she recognized as Brad Gerber and Pete Altman.

"What are they on about?" Edgar murmured.

"I can't tell. Gerber wants to do something and Altman says no, leave that to us."

"Mm." He sounded relieved.

"You know what it means?"

"I haven't the foggiest."

"Edgar, why did you call him? Why are we here?"

He sighed. "I'm afraid push is coming to shove sooner than I'd hoped. Unless someone steps in—"

Through the roses Lydia heard shouts and running footsteps. "Soon, like *now?*"

"Quite possibly."

"Come on then!" She started toward the water.

They were intercepted by an armed officer, who scoffed at Lydia's claim that Detective Altman had been consulting with Mr. Rowdey on this case and urgently wanted to see him.

"Look." Edgar pointed.

A diversion? Lydia poised to make a dash for the boardwalk. Then she followed Edgar's finger. Across the inlet, camouflaged against the salt marsh, a small sailboat sat motionless.

Edgar unsnapped the case around his neck and took out binoculars.

"Becalmed," he confirmed.

"There's been a nice breeze out there since lunchtime," the policeman said accusingly.

Detective Altman came panting up the slope from the dock. "Rosalie Gerber. Went for a sail after her guests left. Hard to blame her, even if . . ." He mopped his forehead with a handkerchief. "What are you two doing here? Collins, did you let them in?"

"Sir—"

"Never mind. Mr. Rowdey, I appreciate your assistance, I really do, but you can't be here. Or you, Ms. Vivaldi. Partly thanks to you, we're now treating this property as a secondary crime scene. So I have to ask you not to get in the way of our investigation."

All three of his listeners spoke at the same time. Officer Collins, nodding toward the house, said: "Detective, you want me to . . .?"

Lydia asked Edgar: "What's he talking about?"

Edgar asked Pete Altman: "You found Miss Benbow's belongings?"

Altman shook his head *no* at Collins and replied to Edgar. "Some of them. We've recovered her watch, and her wallet, with partial contents. We're still looking for her phone and the rest of her jewelry."

"Scattered along the bike path?" Edgar raised his binoculars again.

"That's privileged information." Altman was looking at Lydia.

She blushed and pantomimed zipping her lips.

"Yes," said Altman. "You were right. Now, all that tells us is, someone who had those items in his or her possession tossed them in the bushes. It doesn't mean the same person removed them from the townhouse, or arrived or left via the bike path, or that's who killed Harriet Benbow."

Collins opened his mouth to speak. Lydia hurried in a question. "Have you seen Mudge?"

"He went sailing with Rosalie," Altman said.

"Oh dear heaven." Edgar handed his binoculars to the detective.

Pete Altman focused, grunted in surprise, and watched intently for ten seconds. Then he told Officer Collins, "Find Brad Gerber. Tell him we need to borrow his motorboat." He didn't lower Edgar's binoculars as he slid a phonelike device from his jacket and barked orders in code.

Edgar continued to stare at . . . what?

OK, thought Lydia. The Gerbers do real estate. They're bound to have binoculars.

She ran past the garden and up the steps. Eureka! There was an antique telescope on the porch.

It took her a moment to find the becalmed sailboat. That had to be Rosalie, flaxen-haired in her tennis dress, braced against the mast, struggling with an oar. From here she looked like a white knight trying to maneuver a jousting lance.

Stuck on a sandbar? No. Rosalie swung her oar down over the edge of the boat.

Fighting off a shark attack?

Where the hell was Mudge?

A shout drew Lydia back to the Gerbers' yard. Edgar hadn't moved, but he'd got his binoculars back and aimed at the dinghy. The shout was Detective Altman, racing down the boardwalk to the dock, hollering at Brad Gerber. Behind him thundered Officer Collins.

Too late. Gerber had untied his Boston Whaler. As the policemen closed the gap, he roared off toward his daughter.

Chapter 20: At Sea

Cold water hitting his face slapped Mudge awake. His body was under water. All but his head and one arm. Like an iceberg. His frozen fist clenched on a knot, the end of a rope wrapped around his wrist. The rope's other end ran up to a boat. It must be tied there, or how was it dragging him along like a hooked fish?

He blinked the salt water out of his eyes. Blurry. He made out the top of a mast, with a limp colored sail. No wind.

Where was land? Far away. Little docks, trees, and houses from a model train set.

Over the burbling in his ears he heard splashing.

Rosalie. She'd hit him with an oar. Tried to kill him. She'd knocked him overboard.

Why?

Splash. Drip-drip-drip. Splash.

She must be using the oar to move the boat. Slowly. Paddle a dinghy with one oar? Why?

Did she know he was here?

Should he tell her?

No. This was a crazy woman. Dangerous. She'd pretended to be his friend and his tribe's. She'd vowed to keep her family's promise to give back their land. Then she'd attacked him, screeching like a demon: *I won't let you get away with this!*

Get away with what?

Recovering their stolen burial ground? That made no sense. Two dozen muffins for a golf course—her proposal.

Did she think he murdered Harriet Benbow?

Water in his windpipe was forcing him to cough. *Don't. If she hears you she'll kill you.*

He couldn't help it. His lungs wouldn't let him choose between breathing and choking.

He coughed so hard he had to grab the rope with his other hand. His chest heaved. His eyes wept. His fingers and wrist ached.

The splashing stopped. Over the dinghy's stern, like Moby-Dick, appeared the white hair and white face of Rosalie Gerber.

She didn't hit him. She didn't cut the rope. She said: "I am so sorry."

"Rosalie," he croaked.

"None of this was meant to happen. Harriet. My dad. The land. She kept throwing things off course. I only wanted to make it right."

Mudge couldn't stop coughing. His hand let go of the rope to grope for the boat.

"No!" Rosalie's rubber-soled foot stomped on his fingers. "I can't let you do that."

He forced out words: "What . . .?"

"I saw you figure it out, Mudge. Stupid cops! Two hours, grilling us about cars. The entrance gate. The app on Harriet's phone. Whose car was on the list. Who was in this car and that car that went in and out at this time or that time. But you cut right through that. One look at SailPort Landing and, duh! The bike path!"

He was losing it. He couldn't feel his fingers that were

gripping the knot. Where had his other hand gone?

Rosalie's blowtorch eyes and caterpillar lips commanded him to hang on tight to what she was saying. If he did, would she let him in the dinghy?

". . . golf courses in Mashpee are all burial grounds. Souls depart from bodies the same way they came. Across the sea. Right? So this is the best . . ."

He couldn't do it. The sounds from her mouth flowed around his ears like the cold water sucking at his legs.

Then Rosalie was raising the oar. Mudge's last sensation was a loud bang: the world ending.

➤→

Lydia peered through her telescope. Rosalie Gerber had shifted from whacking the water to dipping into it, like a gondolier.

Where the hell had Mudge disappeared to?

Brad Gerber's Whaler zipped across the inlet, trailing a V of foam. Waterfront acoustics: Rosalie's oar-acrobatics were silent, but the roar of her father's outboard motor carried back to shore. He didn't aim toward the sailboat but out in a wide arc that would take him in front of it. Why? Were moving boats supposed to approach nonmoving ones nose to nose?

Maybe not—Brad was tightening his curve, heading straight at the dinghy, so fast that the Whaler was tilting on its side. *Slow down!* Lydia shouted silently.

He didn't slow down. He rammed straight into the dinghy.

Lydia heard the distant *crack-crunch* of impact, and screams. Altman and the other cop were yelling from the dock. What the hell . . .?

Rosalie dropped her oar and grabbed the mast to keep

from falling overboard. Her arms flailed. The sail flapped. Both boats rocked wildly.

The Whaler's motor must have cut out. Brad Gerber scrambled forward. It took seconds: his boat wasn't much bigger than Rosalie's, barely as long as Leo Harrington's Cadillac. What blocked Lydia's view was its center console and canopy. She strained to see the dinghy and caught only glimpses of white and crimson. The smashed hull? Rosalie's tennis clothes? Brad's red trousers? Blood?

Lydia lowered her telescope. On the dock, Detective Altman and Officer Collins were jogging up the boardwalk. When they reached the Gerbers' yard Collins veered off toward the house next door. Altman continued up the slope, snapping orders into his phone.

Edgar looped his binocular cord around his neck and resumed watching the boats.

Lydia ran down the steps toward him.

"Stop! Police!" someone called.

She didn't look around. She didn't speak to Altman as their paths crossed, or to Edgar as she passed him. She beelined toward the overturned canoe.

"Hey, you! Stop!"

A young Matt Damon lookalike in a cop's uniform was thrashing through the rose garden. Lydia untied the canoe, flipped it into the water, and grabbed two paddles from the trunk.

Officer Ricky Hanlon scrambled into the stern as she pushed off.

"What the hell are you doing? Didn't you hear me?"

"Emergency rescue." She shoved a paddle at him. "You know how to use this? Good. Shut up and paddle."

➤

Officer Hanlon's strength and expertise almost made up for his refusal to stop talking. Lydia needed to understand that he was in charge here. She needed to follow proper procedure for boating accidents. Lydia tuned him out. What she needed was to find some explanation that fit the bizarre scene ahead of them. Two fears obsessed her: Something awful had happened to Mudge, and one or both Gerbers were in it up to their necks.

Ricky Hanlon presented his own problems. Of all the cops on the Exmouth force for Fate to drop into this canoe— She knew from past clashes that he had a hot temper and he didn't like Mudge. If they got there and something awful *had* happened, would he help or make it worse?

Assuming they got there in time to do anything at all . . .

A staticky voice interrupted Officer Hanlon's lecture. He swiveled around so Lydia couldn't eavesdrop and spoke into his shoulder.

The canoe swerved. "Hey!" she snapped.

"Yeah, yeah." With a dismissive wave he steered them back on course. After a brief sotto-voce conference he faced forward again and resumed paddling. "OK. Detective Altman's orders are, proceed with extreme caution. We don't know exactly what the situation is, but we should assume everyone involved is armed and dangerous."

Lydia found this news strangely comforting. So far she'd seen the Gerbers wield a wooden oar and a motorboat. Dangerous maybe, but she didn't think they were armed.

Still, she ducked when a blond head and white shoulders heaved up into sight. Brad? At this distance, riding low in the water, her view blocked by the bobbing Whaler, it was hard to tell. Then she spotted a second blond head. Both of them were moving up and down. Tying the two boats together? The dinghy's limp rainbow sail hung from the broken mast, which slanted like a fishing rod. That looked like a wooden hull drifting back and forth behind the fiberglass Whaler.

"Ahoy!" Officer Hanlon shouted. "Ahoy there!"

The taller head lifted. "Hey," Brad Gerber waved.

He hunched down again, straining to move something or lift something.

"Raise your hands where I can see them!"

Either Brad didn't hear the order or he ignored it. The canoe slowed. Lydia turned. Officer Hanlon was reaching toward his utility belt.

"Don't you dare!" she snapped at him.

Seeing her paddle raised like an axe, he picked up his own. She could hear him muttering into his shoulder radio as they resumed speed.

In less than a minute they reached the Whaler. "Ahoy!" Ricky Hanlon shouted again.

Lydia bellowed: "Where is Mudge?"

Brad Gerber waved them toward the stern, where the round black outboard motor hunched like a goblin. Rosalie, emerging behind him, leaned against the console. She looked battered and exhausted. Yes, that was blood streaking her white tennis outfit. Crimson spots had seeped through the patchwork of gauze pads taped to her legs. A makeshift splint held her left arm stiff under a mummy-wrap of bandages.

"Get the Coast Guard," her father called to Officer Hanlon. "We need help."

Lydia tossed him the rope in the canoe's prow. Brad tied it to a cleat near the engine. If he'd been injured in the crash, it didn't show. She maneuvered past him onto the Whaler before anybody could start playing captain. Behind her Ricky Hanlon was climbing aboard, already barking questions.

The dinghy—what was left of it—floated on the Whaler's starboard side. Its bow and stern pointed up, like a cat's ears. Its middle sagged like a hammock.

No oars in sight.

"Are you OK?" she asked Rosalie. "Where's Mudge?"

Rosalie jerked her head at the bow. She didn't look OK. But Lydia had recognized the dark figure crumpled on the Whaler's foredeck.

Tossing Detective Altman's orders to the vanished wind along with Officer Hanlon's, she stooped beside Mudge.

"He's not dead." Rosalie loomed over her. Lydia peeled back the yellow slicker that covered him from neck to knees. Feeling for a pulse, she took in Mudge's alarmingly cold and swollen hand, his badly abraded wrist, his soaked clothes, his unconscious face, and the ashy pallor of his skin.

Then she saw the blood matting his black hair.

"Blow to the head." Rosalie spoke straight ahead, a zombie. "He almost drowned. My dad gave him CPR. We put him in the sun to get warm."

Lydia stared up at her incredulously. Her expression was as blank as Mudge's.

Behind her, Brad Gerber steered Officer Hanlon to the bench seat at the console.

No chance of privacy here. "Rosalie," Lydia asked anyway, "can you possibly leave us alone for a few minutes?"

She inclined her blonde head half an inch and moved aft.

Lydia glanced at the two men, huddling over Hanlon's shoulder radio. There was a jump seat on this side of the console, and then the flat semicircle in the bow where Mudge lay. Not much she could do but scootch in beside him and turn her back to them. She pulled off Mudge's wet T-shirt, then her own dry one. She wriggled her legs under his head and shoulders. With her T-shirt and her hands she rub-dried every part of him she could reach: his chest, his arms, his neck, and finally his hair.

"Hey!" shouted Officer Hanlon. "Ahoy there!"

He'd stepped onto the narrow strip of deck between the console and the dinghy. He was waving his arms and shouting at an approaching craft: not a bathtub toy like the Gerbers' boats, but a mini-ship with a loud rumbling engine, glassed-in cabin, communications tower, metal railings, and red rubber bumpers: U.S. COAST GUARD.

Lydia felt Mudge's pulse again. Stronger? Or was she refusing to accept the alternative?

One last time she chafed his hands and cheeks. Then she slid out from under him and slithered into her damp blood-smeared T-shirt.

The rescue team eased Mudge onto a stretcher. Lydia forced herself not to hover as they carried him across the shifting gap between boats. He was still out cold, but with an oxygen mask on his face and a thermal blanket tucked around the rest of him. Someone patted her shoulder and told her not to worry. Someone held out a hand as she stepped up onto the Coast Guard boat.

"Hey!" Below her on the Whaler, Officer Hanlon looked around in consternation. "Where's Rosalie?"

Brad Gerber, following Lydia, asked a seaman where he'd find a restroom.

"And where's our canoe?" Hanlon shouted up at him.

One of the Coast Guard crew helped him aboard. Lurching, he grabbed Brad Gerber's elbow. "Sir! Where is your daughter?"

"Excuse me?"

A female crew member called, "You looking for a canoe?"

Everyone on deck hurried around the cabin to join her at the starboard bow. Squinting into the sun, Lydia picked out two silhouettes on the water: a giant floating tin can, and a wild-haired woman paddling a canoe as fast as she could through the inlet's shining mouth into the rip tide of Cape Cod Bay.

Chapter 21: Ashore

Staring at the approaching shoreline from the Whaler, Lydia felt seasick with hatred for Brad Gerber.

Stupid! The one she should hate was Rosalie. Mudge, wrapped in blankets on the jump seat beside her, had croaked out the reason why.

And Lydia did hate Rosalie . . . but not as fiercely, right this minute, as the man standing behind the console with Officer Ricky Hanlon. The father who'd watched his only child face Scylla and Charybdis, and encouraged her to choose a fast death by drowning over the slow torture of a murder trial.

The Coast Guard team who'd revived Mudge had told him not to move from his stretcher until they got him to medical care. When would that be? Officer Hanlon insisted the first priority was to go after Rosalie, who'd paddled out of sight around the point. The skipper insisted his first priority was his rescue mission. Mudge groggily declared he was good to go. Brad Gerber told them to fight it out while he took his Whaler home. In the end Lydia stepped in: unless somebody called a helicopter, the fastest way to get Mudge to medical care was by boat to the Gerbers' house and by road to Cape Cod Hospital.

They compromised. Officer Hanlon radioed to Detective Altman, who said he'd call an ambulance and Hanlon should bring in Brad Gerber for questioning. The skipper ordered two seamen to secure Rosalie's smashed dinghy and one to ferry the civilians across the cove in Brad's Whaler.

With Hanlon and Gerber in the stern, Lydia piloted Mudge to the bow. Their padded seat overlooked the spot where twenty minutes ago—unbeknownst to him—she'd warmed him up. Only when she felt confident he wouldn't pass out or topple over did she swivel to watch the Coast Guard boat head out into Cape Cod Bay.

A scratchy voice beside her whispered: "Rosalie."

"You think they'll find her?" Lydia asked—softly, so the others wouldn't hear.

Mudge's head moved a half inch back and forth.

"Did she explain why . . . ?"

"Not here," he cautioned. And squinted: "Is that Edgar?"

She waited for Officer Hanlon and Brad Gerber to start up the boardwalk before she helped Mudge onto the the little dock. Her heart surged when a familiar white-bearded figure rose from his porch chair, lowered his binoculars, and waved.

Their path toward him was blocked by Detective Pete Altman.

Lydia had hoped the cops would be too busy landing their big fish to remember the small fry. No such luck. After conferring for a moment with Brad Gerber and Officers Hanlon and Collins, Altman pointed them to the house and stepped onto the boardwalk.

"Hey." Flipping up his sunglasses, the detective scanned Mudge from his bandaged head and arms to his dry Coast Guard hoodie and sweat pants. "You doing OK there?"

"Yeah." Lydia could feel him trying not to sag too heavily on her shoulder.

"Your ambulance is on its way. Can you answer a few questions first?"

Mudge coughed. "Yeah."

"The more we can cover now, the less I'll have to pester you tonight at the hospital."

"I'm not . . . staying . . ."

"We need to sit down," Lydia told the detective.

"At the hospital," Mudge rasped.

Altman nodded. He turned away briefly to speak into his phone. Then he took Mudge's other arm, and slowly the three of them inched up the slope.

On the porch, Lydia watched Edgar Rowdey sidle behind the telescope as Brad Gerber strode up the steps and into his house, flanked by Officers Hanlon and Collins.

Their own halting trio was still several yards away when a black-braided young policewoman came out the door carrying two folding chairs. Directed in pantomime by Altman, she set them up on a flat square of lawn near the garden. By the time they reached her, she'd arranged a five-chair circle around a matching table.

Detective Altman piloted Mudge to the nearest seat. "This is Officer Almeida." He stepped back so the young policewoman could set up an audio recorder on the table. "Our tech expert."

Altman beckoned, and Lydia saw Edgar Rowdey traipsing toward them across the patchy grass.

In a low hoarse voice Mudge asked, "What about . . . ?"

"Mr. Gerber? I'll interview him at the station. He's not going anywhere till he confers with his attorney, and you are."

Lydia sat beside Mudge. Edgar took the chair next to hers. Officer Almeida set out a water pitcher and glasses.

"Do I get an attorney?" Mudge croaked.

"Do you want one? You're not accused of anything. This is just to go over what happened out there while it's fresh in your mind." Altman sat on Mudge's other side, close to the table, where he could take notes and see everyone's faces. "OK?"

Edgar leaned in. "Dear, you don't look like yourself at all. How are you feeling?"

Mudge uttered a guttural sound which Lydia recognized as a laugh. "More like me than I did."

Detective Altman told the recorder where they were and who was present. Officer Almeida confirmed the system was working. Altman asked Mudge again if he was OK to answer a few questions. Lydia squirmed with impatience.

"When you were sailing this afternoon with Rosalie Gerber, she assaulted you with an oar. Correct?"

"Yeah."

"Did she say why?"

"She was sorry. She saw I'd figured it out."

"Sorry for what? What had you figured out?"

"The bike path." Mudge cleared his throat and sipped water. "We were near SailPort Landing. She said, the police kept asking about cars. It's shorter by bike."

"Shorter . . . ?"

"From here to Harriet's."

Lydia could almost watch the cogs turning behind Pete Altman's frown. "You mean—" He paused. "Was she talking about Friday night? When Harriet Benbow was fatally attacked?"

Mudge nodded.

"That's a yes," Altman told the recorder. And asked Mudge: "Rosalie Gerber told you that after she and her dad got home, she biked over to the condo at SailPort Landing where Ms. Benbow was staying?"

"Not, like, straight out. But, yeah."

The detective let out a sigh—the sound of an alibi

deflating, thought Lydia. "OK, now, Mudge, I don't want to put words in your mouth. So can you spell this out for me a little clearer?"

Mudge drank more water. "She rode her bike to The Frigate last night. Today on the boat we got talking about the bike path. She thought I put them together and figured out she killed Harriet. Wrong!"

"Did Ms. Gerber admit that to you? 'I killed Harriet Benbow'?"

"No. It was like, no need. Because I already knew. That's why she had to kill me."

"What were her exact words? As best you can recall."

Mudge spoke slowly, replaying it in his mind. "She said, I'm sorry. This wasn't meant to happen. Harriet threw things off course. I had to make it right. The bike path—I saw you figure that out. I can't let you get away with it."

"Aha." There was a pause as Altman mulled this over. "OK. Well, here's my problem, Mudge. It's my job to look at all the possibilities. And what you just said?—doesn't sound like a confession of murder. Indirectly, sure. It could be. No question about that. On the other hand, it could be argued that Ms. Gerber meant she knew you killed her friend, and she intended to make you pay."

"That's crazy!" Lydia protested. "You just saw—"

Altman lifted his hand for silence. "Like, suppose what you figured out was some dirty secret about GreenHome versus the bicycle coalition. Which provoked you to attack Ms. Benbow. Which provoked Ms. Gerber to take you sailing in order to get revenge."

"Mm," Edgar interrupted.

Detective Altman half-turned. "Mr. Rowdey?"

"You mentioned," Edgar said to Mudge, "Rosalie Gerber

biked over to see you at the Frigate. Why? Did she want a book? Or what?"

"She wanted me to bake muffins for her brunch."

"You did that this morning."

"Yeah."

"And this afternoon you went over to pick up your baskets, and she invited you to go sailing?"

"Right."

"How did she seem? Was she angry with you at all? Threatening?"

"No. No. More like . . ."

"More like what?" Pete Altman prodded.

"Interested."

"In your cooking?" Altman asked. Mudge was shaking his head. "What? Your tribe? Your culture?"

"In him!" Lydia exploded. "Jeez!"

Mudge almost snickered. Altman snorted. "OK. Gotcha."

Edgar lifted a bushy white eyebrow at him. "Detective. You're an expert on homicides. Does this sound—"

A faint distant whine sharpened into the wail of a siren.

"Hold that thought," said Altman.

Lydia pushed back her chair, hoping for a moment alone with Mudge on their way out to the street. Instead Detective Altman asked Officer Almeida to escort him.

No problem, she advised herself. Who better to get him into that ambulance than a nice-looking young policewoman?

But don't change the subject, she warned Altman silently. *If you can't follow Edgar's leapfrog logic, you need to stick with him till you catch up.*

"How could Rosalie help liking Mudge?" she prompted. "A thirty-something divorcée, living at home, working for her parents? He's probably the first cool guy she met since her mom got sick. Not like she was, you know. Hunting. It's just been so long, she forgot how to do this."

"What's your point, Ms. Vivaldi?" Detective Altman filled their water glasses.

"So she plays the cards in her hand. You know? Friend of the Wampanoags. Gourmet hostess. Waterfront homeowner with a sailboat." Lydia turned to Edgar. "Right? She didn't plan to kill him. Or Harriet either, probably. She was wound up too tight to think straight. She misread the signals and she panicked."

"Mm," Edgar agreed.

"What is this?" Altman asked. "Female intuition?"

Lydia shot him a withering look. "If you wanted to kill somebody with an oar, would you use the flat side? One whack with the sharp edge . . ."

"He'd be toast," Altman conceded.

"Like Miss Benbow," Edgar said.

"Whoa. How's that?"

"The toastrack," Edgar said with exaggerated patience. "I don't suppose you've had any news yet from the lab?"

"No. I just sent it over this morning. But what's that got to do with Rosalie hitting Mudge with the wrong side of an oar?"

"Heavens to Betsy." Edgar sounded irritated. "Weren't you listening? Everything Mudge told us points in the same direction. This is not a case of a cold-blooded murderer carrying out a plot. Lydia summed it up: Miss Gerber misread the signals, and she panicked."

"Is that so." Detective Altman tone matched Edgar's. "Well now, I'm sure that will be no end of helpful. If we can apprehend her, which I'd say is a long shot, and if we can charge her, which looks even less likely unless the murder weapon pops up, or an eyewitness, or how about a message in a bottle with a confession?"

Lydia looked from him to Edgar and back. "Are we through here?"

"No!" Pete Altman planted his elbows on the table where the recorder sat and ran his hands through his shaggy salt-and-pepper hair. "OK," he said after a moment. "Back up. What about the toastrack?"

"Far be it from me to bias your investigation," said Edgar. "Now that the lab has it, they'll find whatever they find. I suspect that will be Harriet Benbow's blood."

Silence. "Why?" asked Altman.

"You recall I don't know most of these people." Edgar stretched out his legs, bumping the table. "Brad and Rosalie Gerber. Mudge's two cousins, the chief and the council chairman. Harriet Benbow. I rely on the people I do know. You two, Mudge, Leo and Tony, Mrs. French, a few others. Leo wheedled me into this when you went after Tony. Poor bunny! I never imagined for an instant he was capable of slaughtering a woman with a toastrack."

Detective Altman sat up straight. "What?"

"I told you this morning. This hoo-hah always revolved around the toastrack. Solve that enigma and the rest of the puzzle would fall into place."

"Remind me. What enigma?"

Edgar sighed. "Friday morning. Tony Harrington drives Rosalie Gerber and Harriet Benbow around Quansett. They stop at a yard sale. Tony and Rosalie squabble—flirtatiously—over a silver toastrack. Harriet snatches it out from under their noses."

"You snooze, you lose," said Lydia.

"Well, exactly. Not the friendliest of messages from a

former therapist to a former client. One can only wonder if Rosalie recognized it then as the warning it was. In any event, onward they tootled to lunch at Leo's. Hosted by Tony, ably catered by Lydia and Mudge. Tony's aim was for GreenHome LLC to hire him as an expediter for SailPort Landing. Harriet I gather scuppered that hope, along with the Wampanoags' hope that GreenHome would finally deed over their burial ground in Mashpee. She intended the company to move on. Sell the condos, donate the salt marsh, and develop every inch of the old golf course. All she needed was an OK from Brad Gerber."

Noises from the house reminded Detective Altman of the other fish he still had to fry. "You mind cutting to the chase?"

"Oh, I am, believe me," said Edgar. "Friday afternoon. Tony's lunch guests and their plans scattered to the four winds. Tony grasped at one last straw with a bottle of exceptional Scotch. He would swing by the townhouse where Ms. Benbow was staying to bribe or seduce her into reconsidering. He'd realized at lunch that for her, this weekend dedicated to Lanie Gerber's memory was a chance to jump into Lanie Gerber's shoes. With both feet, as you might say. Tony had faith in his personal charms to give him leverage. He failed to realize that Ms. Benbow had already used that leverage to provoke Brad Gerber into proposing marriage."

"He misread the signals," breathed Lydia.

"Who?" Pete Altman put in. "Tony? Or Brad? Or are we back to Rosalie?"

"All of them," said Edgar. "That's the tragedy of it. Two lives cut short, one hair's-breadth escape, and a swath of destruction in their wake, because they misread the signals."

Chapter 22: Jetsam

Any minute, Lydia thought, Brad Gerber will slam open that door and T-bone this conversation like he rammed Rosalie's boat.

"All of them?" she echoed. "Including Harriet?"

"Mm," Edgar affirmed. "Q.E.D."

"You want to spell that out for me?" said Detective Altman.

"As events have shown, Miss Benbow apparently had a gift for seizing her moment, coupled with a fatal weakness for getting hold of the wrong end of the stick."

"Meaning what in plain English?"

"She overestimated her influence at GreenHome. With both Gerbers, but disastrously with Rosalie."

Edgar sighed and sat back, wriggling to get comfortable. Detective Altman pressed on.

"So you're convinced Rosalie Gerber killed Harriet Benbow."

"Oh yes." Edgar's chair squeaked. "Until this afternoon I wondered—but the way she went after Mudge leaves no room for doubt."

"You wondered what?"

"Her father I can't help feeling has acted oddly. Heaven knows I haven't the remotest idea why anyone ever marries anyone, let alone how they choose to go about it. I'm assured, though, it is not customary to court one's late wife's assistant at her memorial party with a ring hot off her cold dead finger."

Pete Altman stifled a snort. "You've been talking to Louise French."

"I'm also assured that Brad Gerber is not easily flustered. Any second thoughts, he'd have found a way out of his commitment short of murder."

"Did you wonder at all if this was a botched burglary? That was Louise's theory. And Tony Harrington's."

"It's the pet theory of your whole suspect list," Lydia put in. "Accidental murder by a drug-crazed addict looking for loot. That went down the hole when your guys found Harriet's wallet and her watch."

"Oh, long before then," Edgar said. "It didn't fit the crime."

"What about the Wampanoags?" Altman asked. "Did you consider any of them?"

"Mudge's cousins? No way," Lydia said positively.

"Mr. Rowdey? You never thought they'd fight to stop Ms. Benbow from developing their burial ground in Mashpee?"

Edgar sighed and examined a scab on his thumb.

"I'm not accusing anybody," Altman added. "Only, you know Lanie Gerber did promise that land to the tribe."

"Speculation won't get the baby bathed," said Edgar. "Detective, I appreciate your wish to be thorough. However! The fact remains, Harriet Benbow was killed by Rosalie Gerber. Even if we hadn't just seen her admit it, in deeds if not words, there was no one else at Tony's lunch who matches the three criteria for this crime. That includes the host, the caterers, and the phantom burglar."

"Three criteria." Pete Altman flipped a page in his notebook. "Your toastrack, and what are the other two?"

"I was speaking of motive, means, and opportunity. But since you ask. One, the toastrack. Two, access. I doubt Miss Benbow unlocked her door for anyone she wasn't expecting or didn't recognize. As for how an outsider could have got into SailPort Landing other than by the gate, I know only what Mudge just told us regarding the bike path."

"We'll have more on that tomorrow," said Altman, scribbling notes. "Three?"

"The scalping."

"A frame-up," Lydia said. "Obviously."

Edgar lifted an eyebrow. "Of the Wampanoags? By Rosalie Gerber?"

"Huh." Detective Altman looked up. "Interesting point. I can almost make a case for Rosalie killing her friend to stop her developing land GreenHome promised to the Indians. But, frame the Indians for the murder?" He scratched his head with his pen. "What do you figure? Was she pointing us to the Wampanoags? Or is it not about that? Is this whole scalping thing a red herring? Why did Rosalie rip off Harriet's hairpiece? Assuming she did."

Lydia, hearing voices in the hall, said, "She must have. Who else could, or would?"

"Mm," Edgar agreed. "As for *why*, I haven't the foggiest notion."

The screen door slammed open.

"I can help you with that," said Brad Gerber.

He stepped onto the porch and stood looming over the little table. Wet curls of straw-colored hair stuck to his sweaty forehead; dry tufts bristled above his ears. Under the ruddiness of sunburn his face looked pallid.

"Will you join us, Mr. Gerber?" Detective Altman half-rose.

"Sure." He took the chair Officer Almeida had left.

"You got hold of your attorney?"

Ricky Hanlon, standing in the doorway, mouthed *yes*.

"Stuart Redbone. Yes. I filled him in on . . . recent events. I told him, as I understand it, I may be charged with assault with a deadly weapon. He advised me not to discuss that with you until he meets us at the station in an hour."

"Right. OK then."

"I told him, all right, but I want to make a statement regarding my daughter."

Lydia froze. Edgar went on picking at the scab on his thumb.

"Thank you, sir. I appreciate that." Altman pushed back his chair. "Shall we?"

"Here," said Brad Gerber. "On my own property. You're set up to record, right? That's my one condition. I want to speak here, at my family's home."

Officer Hanlon moved one hand to his utility belt. Pete Altman shook his head warningly.

"We scattered some of my wife's ashes right over there. A private ceremony in her garden at dawn. Harriet and Rosalie and me. Two days ago. Hard to believe. The rest we sent out to sea yesterday in a little wooden sailboat."

Ricky Hanlon, still on guard in the doorway, glanced around as if to make sure Rosalie hadn't sneaked back and hidden nearby.

"Edgar Rowdey, isn't it?" Gerber inquired. "Will you be a witness? And the young lady who came out to help."

"Lydia Vivaldi," said Detective Altman.

"Pleasure." Gerber held out his hand. After two seconds' hesitation Lydia took it, not wishing to risk her seat at the table. GreenHome's CEO had a firm grip and cold fingers. Did he recognize her from lunch at Leo's? She couldn't tell. He looked so shell-shocked, maybe he couldn't either.

"Detective Pete Altman of the Exmouth Police Department speaking to Mr. Bradford Gerber at his home in Quansett. Mr. Gerber, you've offered to help us by making a voluntary statement."

"That's right." He wiped his forehead with the back of his hand.

"I cautioned him upstairs," Offer Hanlon interjected.

"I want to report a conversation I had with my daughter Rosalie aboard our Boston Whaler. An hour ago? You were here, detective; you'll have the time. I'll just say, the last time I saw her."

Ricky Hanlon leaned in toward the recorder. "The Coast Guard is continuing their search for Rosalie Gerber in Cape Cod Bay."

"Thank you, Officer Hanlon. Will you . . .?" Detective Altman waved at him to go join the team of cops who were poking through the marsh grass alongside the boardwalk.

"They won't find her," Brad Gerber said tightly. "They said they have to try. I told them it's pointless. Whatever her intentions were—"

He stopped. "Sorry. Just report my conversation with my daughter. So. Do you want to go back to your question when I came out here? Harriet's hair? Or start at the beginning?"

Pete Altman looked at Edgar Rowdey.

"Oh, start at the beginning, by all means," said Edgar.

"They met in Cambridge, must be five or six years ago. Harriet was Rosalie's therapist. She helped her through the breakup of her marriage and the loss of her job. That's one reason why my wife and I relocated GreenHome's office to Sandwich. It's close to the bridge, so Rosalie could commute back and forth until things settled down." Gerber recited these facts without emotion. "After her divorce she joined us full-time and moved in here. She and Harriet stayed friends, and when Lanie's cancer came back, Rosalie asked if Harriet still thought of changing careers. From counseling to real estate. It worked out better than we hoped. Harriet started part-time, as my wife's assistant, and moved up to business manager."

"Harriet Benbow joined GreenHome when?" Pete Altman asked.

"Year and a half ago. Detective, I understand you have questions, but if you'll let me get through my statement."

"Sure."

"We've always been a small, tight company, and we've done very well. Lanie had a phenomenal eye. She could look at five acres of scrub oak or a derelict shopping mall, size up the context, and say *Thirty-six units of mixed-income housing with a community garden*, or, *Two stories around a central court-yard*. When we got her diagnosis, her biggest fear was leaving loose ends. She was able to tie them all up except for SailPort Landing and the Mashpee golf course."

"The Wampanoag burial ground," Lydia murmured.

"The damn goalposts kept moving. Wetlands restrictions and tribal sovereignty. Lanie thought we were home free when the tribe's reservation went through and Harriet grandfathered in our three model condos. We can do this! Almost. We lost her too soon. I had to step away from GreenHome toward the end. I had to be with Lanie. Rosalie too. But Harriet hung on for all of us. Thank God, I thought. A steady hand at the helm. I didn't realize . . ." He paused. "I didn't know until today that Rosalie minded."

"She told you out there on the Whaler?" Pete Altman asked.

"The last thing I wanted was to hurt my daughter." Brad Gerber planted his forearms on the table with a thump of fists that rattled the recorder. "She felt betrayed, she said. Pushed aside. I had no idea! But things were changing so fast." He grimaced. "It was for Rosalie's sake I agreed to that lunch with Tony Harrington. I thought, here's a decent guy who obviously likes her. Always flirting. She told me I got it wrong. Tony had switched to Harriet, figuring she'd be an easier conquest. Rosalie thought that's why Harriet slept at the Ketch, was to sneak around with Tony. Until she turned on him. Turned on both of them when they were driving around Quansett Friday morning and stopped at a yard sale."

After several seconds Lydia said, "You mean the toast-rack?"

Brad Gerber looked at her in mild surprise, as if he'd forgotten she was there. "Yes. They all saw the thing, they squabbled over it, and Harriet grabbed it. And mocked the losers."

Again he fell silent for a moment. Then, checking his watch, he continued.

"That was her warning shot, Rosalie told me. For the bomb she dropped at lunch. Moving SailPort Landing from Quansett to Mashpee. I thought Harriet made it clear this was just an idea, a discussion point. We run GreenHome by consensus. Always. But Rosalie said, that's not what she heard. Friday night at dinner, Harriet showed us on the plot plan how the project could fit into the space. When I didn't say no, Rosalie took it as a done deal. She had no idea Harriet and I had just gotten engaged. She was still spooked by that business at the yard sale."

He drew in a breath and let it out. "After we got home, Rosalie rode her bike over to the Ketch. I was playing pool with our guests; I didn't hear her go. She told me today, Harriet opened the door but wouldn't let her in. She didn't want to talk. Least of all about GreenHome. Rosalie said she smelled of liquor. There was a bottle of Scotch on the kitchen island, and that toastrack thing sitting beside it. Rosalie pushed her way in, and Harriet poured her a drink. And Rosalie saw that she was wearing Lanie's ring."

His voice broke. He cleared his throat and resumed.

"This was an emerald-and-diamond ring that I put on Lanie's finger thirty-five years ago when she agreed to be my wife. It's been in my family for generations. It would have gone to Rosalie after Lanie died if she'd still been married. Harriet was fine with that. She said she would give it to Rosalie if she ever married again. For now, it was important to Harriet as a sign of joining our family. We agreed she wouldn't wear it in public until we told Rosalie our good news and the three of us could make the announcement together."

Pete Altman was scribbling in his notebook as if he didn't dare look up.

"Rosalie said, when she saw it, something exploded. She screamed at Harriet: *Give back my mother's ring!* And Harriet laughed. *Grow up!* Rosalie threw her drink in Harriet's face. Harriet picked up the toastrack. *Here. You can have this instead. My wedding present to you.* And Rosalie said: I took it and I hit her with it. I didn't mean to. Everything just went red. I hit her and hit her and she fell. Her head caught on the kitchen island. The granite edge. And this big handful of hair came loose. I thought, Omigod! But it was fake! Like everything else about her. So I ripped it off all the way. To take home and show my dad. What a horrible mistake he made—we both made—"

With his elbows on the table, Brad Gerber buried his face

in his hands.

"OK," Pete Altman said evenly. "OK now."

Edgar Rowdey spoke with uncharacteristic sharpness. "Mr. Gerber. Please tell Detective Altman why the Coast Guard can't save your daughter."

The answer came in a muffled voice. "It's too late."

"Why?" Altman asked.

"Lanie's pain pills. She never took them. She wanted her mind clear." Brad Gerber's elbows were sliding slowly apart, his pale head sagging. "We put them in the Whaler's first-aid kit."

"You're saying Rosalie took those pills?" The detective scrambled to his feet.

"She took her half." His face hit the table.

"Officer Hanlon!" Altman waved. "Call an ambulance!"

Chapter 23: Landing

The wind rose as Edgar and Lydia drove home, bringing clouds which thickened and darkened the azure sky to bruise-colored purple. By the time his VW wagon bumped through the gap in the hedge, the sun had disappeared. There would be fog on the roads within hours, he predicted. Not a good night to dine out. We can call each other if either of us hears any news.

Not likely, thought Lydia. Who'd have fresher news than us? The cops? The Coast Guard? The emergency room?

Edgar would no doubt call Leo with the news that Tony was off Detective Altman's suspect list. Lydia called Mudge and got voicemail. Figuring he'd been fussed over enough for one night, she left a message asking if he'd be at work tomorrow.

A noise like bacon crackling woke her early from bad dreams. Rain. For half a minute she took slow breaths and watched drops exploding on her skylight. Drive to the Back End? No. She needed to stretch her legs. Fill her lungs with damp fresh air before suffocating them with burger grease and Pine-Sol.

Less than a day since Mudge borrowed Leo's kitchen to bake muffins for Rosalie Gerber. How long since we catered Tony's business luncheon?

In her head Brad Gerber answered: *Two days. Hard to believe.*

No. Sunday, Saturday, Friday . . . three days.

Still too soon to go back there.

Shockingly, none of the Back End customers seemed aware that over the weekend a chunk of their village had flipped and split open like the eggs on Dinah's grill.

Lydia surreptitiously checked the *Cape Cod Times*. Not a word about the Fall of the House of Gerber. The regulars at the counter, comparing sound bites from this morning's TV news, didn't mention it.

"Where's Mudge?" she asked Dinah.

"Late. Headache. He said he'll be here before Leo comes down. So move your butt. I got three Egz Bennie waiting for toast."

Placing English muffins on Leo's antique revolving toaster, Lydia shut out the vision that had haunted her all night: Harriet Benbow's laughing face crumpled into horror by the jabbing point of a silver Art Deco toastrack.

Seven-thirty. Eight o'clock. Eight-thirty. Even with the breakfast crowd shrunk by the weather, even with Tony delivering plates and making coffee whenever he could leave the register, Lydia struggled. She kept glancing at the doorway, but Mudge didn't appear.

Neither did Edgar Rowdey's yellow slicker.

Finally she asked Tony: "What's happened to Edgar?"

"You got me," he shrugged. "You were there last night?"

"Yeah."

"Let me ask you—"

"Later."

Ten. Ten-thirty. Where was Edgar? Where was Mudge? Still in the hospital? Stranded on the road between Mashpee and Quansett with a broken-down pickup truck and a concussion?

If anyone knew, it would be Leo. Dinah had left him a brusque phone message: we're short-staffed, it's your restaurant, get your ass down here. So where the hell was Leo?

"Hey," Dinah beckoned. "Phone call."

Lydia picked up as Leo made his entrance. He had an uncanny knack for descending from his apartment just when the lull hit between breakfast and lunch. Fingers crossed, he'd be too busy snarking with customers to bust her for using the house phone.

"Mudge? Are you OK? Where are you?"

"I'm out front. Edgar wants to talk to you. Can you sneak out when I come in?"

She hated to miss her first chance to talk to Mudge, but they couldn't both take the same break. Edgar's parking lights glowed a welcoming yellow through the rain. Lydia slithered into his passenger seat.

"What's going on?" she demanded.

"Oh, the usual this and that. Mudge and I ran into each other at police headquarters. They'd sent a car to the hospital for him. Our friend Mr. Altman summoned me to the station to tie up a few loose ends, and he kindly took me to breakfast. I felt the least I could do on behalf of all concerned was give Mudge a ride."

"Are you coming inside?"

"It's barely eleven, dear. I'll be back at lunchtime. I know you can't stay. I wanted to tell you outside the public eye, they found Rosalie Gerber's canoe."

Lydia felt as if she'd been punched in the stomach. That's why he asked me to come out here, she realized. Edgar understands it doesn't really matter if you knew or liked the person, or even if you believe an eye for an eye is justice. This is not news you want to hear when you're trying to serve customers.

"Only her canoe?" she had to ask.

"So far. Very likely ever, Detective Altman said. Currents and tides and so forth. Canoes are buoyant. It was floating upside down."

"Is the Coast Guard still searching?"

"Oh, I shouldn't think so. Missing Presumed Dead. You recall her father's statement. If they each took half of the late Mrs. Gerber's pills, the medical examiner said Rosalie would have lost consciousness fairly quickly."

Lydia let out a long gasping sigh.

Edgar's eyes were on his windshield wipers, ticking back and forth like a metronome. "Brad Gerber didn't survive his trip to the hospital," he answered her unspoken question.

They were silent for a moment. "I'd better get back," said Lydia.

"Mm."

"You know, nobody's talking about any of this yet," she said. "Not the media, not even the grapevine."

"One small blessing to be thankful for." He wriggled his shoulders. "The police are zipping ahead with their investigation. Hoping to close the case before it hits the fan, I expect. Someone at HQ was promoting a theory to the effect that Miss Benbow slipped and fatally hit her head on an unfinished countertop, causing her dear friend Miss Gerber to become unhinged with grief when she sailed past the site of the tragedy, whereupon her father dashed to her rescue and perished in the attempt."

Lydia, opening the car door, said, "I'm guessing that wasn't Detective Altman."

"Ta-ta till lunchtime," said Edgar.

➤➤

In the Back End's kitchen, other things were hitting the fan.

Leo, shocked by his patrons' ignorance of recent events, had seized the opportunity to enlighten them. He didn't see why Mudge wouldn't cooperate. Or why he insisted on wearing that funny cap that made him look like a drug dealer. Mudge didn't see why Leo wouldn't leave him alone to do his job. Tony elbowed in to remind everyone in earshot that this was an ongoing murder investigation and therefore fell under Detective Altman's warning about loose lips. Leo snapped back that Mudge here was the expert on sinking ships, and why should their friends in the police community care if he shared a little information? Dinah hollered from the kitchen that if Leo didn't shut up and give Lydia a hand, and Tony didn't cash out those two families waiting by the register, she'd broil their buns with a blowtorch.

Lydia caught up with Mudge fifteen minutes later. He was spooning Choklit Moose into dessert glasses. Without a word she squirted a whipped-cream rosette onto each one.

"They kept you at the hospital?" she asked when he opened the maraschino cherries.

"Overnight," he nodded. "The doctor told me about this actress who hit her head skiing and sent away the ambulance and she died from internal bleeding. But they couldn't stop me going to the police station this morning." He speared a cherry. "That sucks about Rosalie's dad."

"Yeah."

"She told me on the boat: him and her mom were so tight, she felt like there was never any room for her." A crimson drop fell on the white mound below. "I guess it made her crazy how fast he made room for Harriet."

"I can't believe—" Lydia started, and stopped.

"What?"

That she killed her best friend and almost killed you, over him.

"That he smashed her boat with her in it," she said instead. "His own daughter."

"Saved my life." Mudge handed her a tray. "Back room. Three each, Tables Two and Five."

Edgar appeared shortly after noon. The rain must have stopped. He'd shed his yellow slicker, and he'd brought a guest: a suburban-elegant blonde lady in a multicolored jacket, linen slacks, and designer heels.

"Louise French!" Leo met her at the door, taking both her hands in his. "Welcome to our humble establishment. I've got a booth in the back room with your name on it."

He turned to sling his usual greeting insults at Edgar, but Edgar had veered off to speak to Mudge.

Mudge delivered their lunch: Greek Sallid for Mrs. French and Chix Pot Pi for Edgar. At their request (Lydia assumed) he lingered by their booth. His back was to the room, so all she could tell was that Louise French was doing most of the talking. Lydia saw her pale fingers rest on Mudge's brown forearm above his food-spattered bandages.

A few minutes later Mudge came and found Lydia in the soup corner, stirring the clam chowder.

His eyes were bright as if he were holding back tears. "What was that about?" she asked.

"She's the realtor who found Harriet Benbow's body. She was helping GreenHome with those three townhouses. She said—" Mudge paused. "Edgar told her what happened yesterday. She thought I'd want to know Brad and Lanie Gerber signed a paper to give the Wampanoag burial ground back to the tribe."

Mudge looked almost as stunned as when she'd found him yesterday on Brad Gerber's Whaler. "What does that mean exactly?" asked Lydia.

"It's like, legally in writing. Harriet's idea that she talked about at Tony's lunch, to switch SailPort Landing to Mashpee? Mrs. French said Brad Gerber was all for it, like if the tribe wanted GreenHome to develop some of the land for housing or whatever, but it wasn't his decision. It was totally up to the tribe."

Lydia glanced over at the booth. Leo was joking with Edgar and Mrs. French, refilling their coffee cups.

"Did your cousins know that?"

"No! Not for sure," Mudge amended. "The Gerbers promised. They'd do a ceremony as soon as the status and the reservation and the casino thing got sorted out. But, you know, people have been promising for hundreds of years. I was afraid . . ." He shook his head in its knitted cap.

"How sure is Mrs. French?"

Mudge flashed a shaky grin. "A hundred percent. Oh, here comes Leo." And before she could hug him in congratulations, he took off for the kitchen.

➤

Edgar also took off before Lydia was through with him. For once she skipped the usual formalities when she got home from work. Without phoning to see if he were free, without even showering off the day's grease and perspiration, she marched up the weathered porch steps to his door.

"Hul-lo," he answered her knock. "I thought that would

be you."

"The Wampanoags are getting their land back. How did you know?"

Edgar stepped onto the porch. "I asked," he said smugly.

"Out of all the people in Quansett—"

"I ran into Louise French yesterday, if you'll recall. I'd been fretting over the toastrack enigma, and it occurred to me she might have some light to throw." He pushed up his glasses and looked down his nose. "I do have a deadline, you know."

"A deadline?"

"For 'The Toastrack Enigma.' The story I recklessly agreed to write and illustrate for *Golden Age Mysteries*?"

"Oh, right. Of course. How could that have slipped my mind?" Lydia sat on the porch railing. "So, did you get it back?"

"Did I get what back?"

"Your toastrack. Harriet Benbow's toastrack. Rosalie Gerber's toastrack."

"The Exmouth Police Department's toastrack. No, certainly not. If the forensic people ever finish with it, I dare-say it will vanish into some vast evidence-storage warehouse till the end of time."

He looked untroubled, standing in his wet green bower of clematis vines. "How will you finish your story without your MacGuffin?" she asked him.

"Oh, I'll manage. It's played its part. Gave me a title, strutted its hour upon the stage, and left me with a zippier plot than I could have thought up myself on such short notice." Edgar dodged a dangling tendril. "A week ago I was inching toward a lawn party. Now I've got the Right Honourable Tiberia Wormbold setting her cap for Sir James Dropthmore, recently widowed, at the annual jumble sale for St-Hildebrand-on-Marsh, where they stumble upon a silver toastrack with a shady past."

"Is this based on any persons or utensils we know?"

"My lips are sealed. The innocent rarely recognize them-selves, and the guilty can't press charges."

Lydia felt the damp wood soaking through her jeans. "Does Sir James have a daughter?"

"I'm toying with a suggestion Mrs. French made." He twined the tendril around his finger. "He has a daughter who's willing to forgive him everything, but he can't forgive her anything. Thus dooming them both."

"Like Lear and Cordelia." Lydia got to her feet.

"Mm. Lear and Cordelia with a toastrack, as reimagined by Agatha Christie."

"I can't wait to read it."

"Dear, you'll have to. I haven't written it yet."

The rain was starting again. "Time for me to go get clean before the heavens step in."

"More showers forecast tomorrow," said Edgar. "Hard on Detective Altman, herding his ducks into a row."

Lydia peered out at the gray sky. "Oh. That reminds me."

Edgar had let go of the clematis vine, which swayed gently beside his head. "Of what?" She could see his mind was already climbing the stairs to his drawing table, girding for battle with his story.

"What about the other MacGuffin? The poison pill in the GreenHome tragedy. Lanie Gerber's ring."

"Ah yes. Well, of course I don't know. Mudge said Rosalie wasn't wearing it. Naturally Mr. Altman's people have begun looking through her things, and they didn't find it. On the other hand, one can't picture her hurling it into the marsh with Harriet Benbow's wallet and cell phone."

"No," said Lydia.

"If I were Rosalie Gerber—"

Their eyes met. For the first time in their acquaintance, Lydia knew what Edgar Rowdey was thinking before he uttered the words.

She spoke first.

"The rose garden. Buried with her mother's ashes."

"Well, exactly," said Edgar.

If you've enjoyed *Shafted, or The Toastrack Enigma:
an Edgar Rowdey Cape Cod Mystery,*

PLEASE

post a review on Amazon, Goodreads, or another
book site you like;
ask your local library to order it;
give it to someone—in paperback from any local or online
bookstore, or as an ebook;
read the other books and stories in this series
(see below).
More information at https://Boom-Books.com

About the Author

C J Verburg is an award-winning playwright, director, and author of best-selling books, including the international literature collections *Ourselves Among Others* and *Making Contact*. Along with two series of contemporary Golden Age mystery novels (see below), she's published a number of short stories, including "Scandal at the Savoy: The Monocle Murder" in the October 2021 Sherlock Holmes issue of *Mystery Magazine* and the Edgar Rowdey story "A Terrible Tragedy" in Malice Domestic's 2021 anthology *Mystery Most Diabolical.*

A longtime neighbor, friend, and collaborator of the artist and writer Edward Gorey, CJ produced and assistant-directed most of his dozen-plus theatrical "entertainments" on Cape Cod. You can read about their thespian adventures, and enjoy rare drawings and photos, links to film clips, even music, in ***Edward Gorey On Stage: Playwright, Director, Designer, Performer: a Multimedia Memoir.***

For more about CJ's books, plays, and personal history, *see* http://cjverburg.net or https://Boom-Books.com.

Edward Gorey On Stage: Playwright, Director, Designer, Performer: A Multimedia Memoir

From his boyhood he was fascinated by theater. Once he got out of the Army, Edward Gorey's escapades onstage and backstage kept him entertained for the rest of his life.

"*Edward Gorey On Stage* is a thoroughly enjoyable publication chronicling Edward Gorey's theatrical career . . . [particularly] on and around Cape Cod in the 1980s and '90s. Ms. Verburg was a hands-on participant (or co-conspirator) in most of these endeavors, and she has many stories to delight the Gorey enthusiast." — *Irwin Terry, Goreyana*

". . . Packed with detail and insight into Edward Gorey the playwright, director and performer . . . I come out feeling like an insider." — *Glen Emil, Goreyography*

". . . A joy to read. . . I especially loved the multimedia links . . . that you can scan with your phone—it's like getting a second multimedia companion volume. It's a must have for fans of Gorey's work but it's also a fantastic example of the "in the trenches" process of developing theater pieces . . . for anyone interested in the performing arts. — *Paul M, Amazon*

"The book is a gem for those of us who did the stuff and . . . the audiences who experienced the most radical theater to be done on Cape Cod." — *Eric H. Edwards, actor & poet*

"A must have for every follower of the late theatrical artist Edward Gorey, this book . . . describes his work on his 20-plus plays: odd, sweet, cruel, sad, nostalgic, incomprehensible and enchanting . . . "— *MGB, Amazon*

Croaked: an Edgar Rowdey Cape Cod Mystery (#1)

Is the charming seaside town of Quansett a sanctuary or a death trap? It takes a village to find out—led by an urban refugee and a reclusive artist.

"Everything I want in a mystery: wonderful kooky characters, a plot that keeps you turning pages, terrific dialog, humor, great local color, . . . oh yes, and murders, too. I enjoyed every minute of it. Highly recommended!" — *SW, Amazon*

"A real page-turner with many moving pieces, wonderfully fey characters, and delightful surprises throughout. Great Cape Cod color, terrific fun, and a must for anyone who loves to curl up with a good mystery." — *CC, Goodreads*

"A thoroughly enjoyable murder mystery . . . Plot, characters, and setting combine for enough twists and turns to keep readers guessing, and reading. Highly recommended." — *CW, Goodreads*

Zapped: an Edgar Rowdey Cape Cod Mystery (#2)

If inventor Pam Nash is right about Zappa,
it could revolutionize law enforcement.
If she's wrong, they'll kill her daughter.

"I loved *Zapped.* . . . The plotting is clever in the manner of the gentle mysteries of the mid 20th century golden age that mixed good writing with humour and a dab of irony." —*JB, Goodreads*

" . . . Enjoyed it from the dazzling opening to the twist at the end. . . . Highly recommended for people who like a little edge on their cozies." — *P, Amazon*

"Interesting characters who hold your attention throughout this intriguing mystery set in summertime Cape Cod. I look forward to another by this author." —*AL, Goodreads*

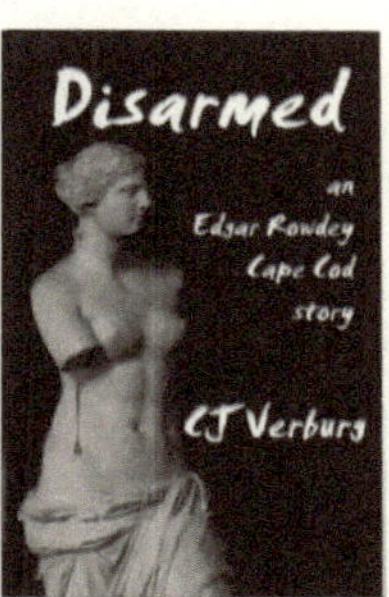

FREE! Disarmed: an Edgar Rowdey Cape Cod story
(details at https://Boom-Books.com or http://cjverburg.net)

Sample from Page 1:

What's happened to Freddy Coughlin?

He was only supposed to unlock the gate to the garbage bins for the truck. When he hasn't come back after fifteen minutes, Lydia Vivaldi slips out to look for him.

The sun warms her bare head and arms as she rounds the corner of Leo's Back End. It's the kind of sparkling Cape Cod morning when she can hear birds singing in the woods out back of the restaurant and imagine how the sand would feel under her feet if she hopped on her bike and made a dash for the beach. As she crosses the damp grass toward the stockade fence, dew soaks through her sneakers.

Freddy started working here four days ago. Leo balked at giving him a job, never mind that it's tourist season and his staff can use the help. Freddy married Leo's daughter Jackie. After six weeks of searching she put her foot down: nobody else is gonna hire him, even though he's paid his debt to society, and for God's sake, it was only weed and pills, not meth or heroin or crack like those gang-bangers over in Hyannis, and if his own father-in-law won't lend him a hand, then who the hell will?

Silent Night Violent Night: a Cory Goodwin Mystery

A publisher's Christmas party. A blizzard. Rival scientists.
Secret romances. Murder.

"Captures you from the first sentence and keeps you 'hooked' until the last period!" — *KF, Amazon*

". . . Worth crossing New England in a blizzard to get to read this . . . murder mystery / hold-onto-your-pants thriller. . . . Enough twists, ducks and dives to make Agatha Christie self-exhume." — *CH, Amazon*

"Great characters, lots of conflict, and wry insights into the effects of commerce on...scholarship make this a great read. And no, I did NOT guess the ending, even though the clues were there." — *CPL, Amazon*

(from Chapter 1)

As I swung out of Copley Square onto the Mass Pike, the band on my radio swung into "Hernando's Hideaway." Desultory snowflakes were drifting through the orange sky like petals. Half an inch, the weatherman predicted. I'd picked this station because Oxbridge, Connecticut, is a three-hour drive from Boston and the rest were all playing Christmas songs.

Another Number for the Road: a Cory Goodwin Mystery

Why is Boston's notorious rock-protest guitarist and
murder suspect coming back after 20 years
to play for an upscale trip to Paris?

The first literary rock-&-roll mystery with a live soundtrack.

"With all of the twist and turns of a great mystery, *Another Number for the Road* takes the reader for a ride into an intimate world of power, intrigue, and rock & roll . . . In short, a winner." — *CI, Amazon*

"The music is exhilarating, the romance is hot, and the mystery is challenging. A perfect book for summertime reading even if you can't get to Paris." — *AF, Amazon*

"A fun great read. The author sets the atmosphere perfectly, and . . . has also cleverly found a way for the reader to actually listen to the fictional band's music!" — *HR, Goodreads*

(from Chapter 1)

The swan boats in the Public Garden were tied up for the night, and the Goodyear blimp was nosing toward Fenway Park, when I walked between two seven-foot gold lions into the Faneuil Plaza Hotel.

Across the street behind me stood a glass tower topped by the notorious penthouse where my onetime idol Mickey Ascher died. Past that was the river-view condo where I'd been holed up since January.

Two provocations had brought me here on this balmy spring evening. One was the invitation in my purse:

Please join Hands Across the Sea, 7 PM Friday, June 3. An Adventure in International Good Will!

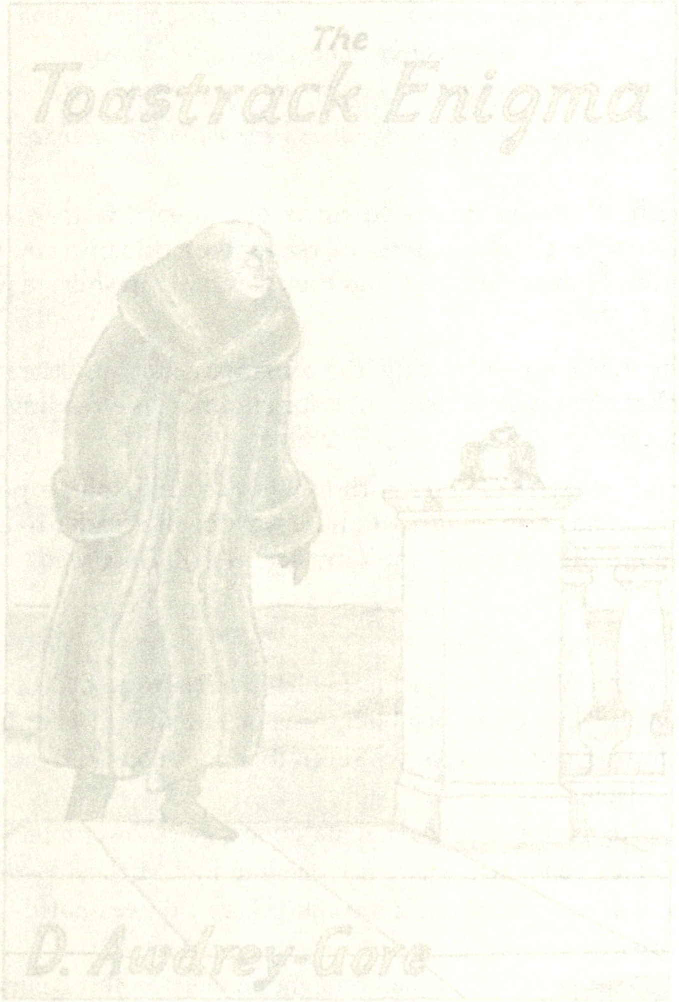

The
Toastrack Enigma

D. Awdrey-Gore